REAP
THE
STORM

SIEGFRIED LANGER

REAP THE STORM

Translated by Jaime McGill

amazoncrossing

Previously published as *Vergelte!* by Amazon Publishing in Germany in 2015. Translated from German by Jaime McGill. First published in English by AmazonCrossing in 2015.

Published by AmazonCrossing, Seattle

www.apub.com

Amazon, the Amazon logo, and AmazonCrossing are trademarks of Amazon.com, Inc., or its affiliates.

ISBN-13: 9781503949812
ISBN-10: 1503949818

Cover design by Edward Bettison

Printed in the United States of America

"I the Lord your God am a jealous God, visiting the iniquities of the fathers upon the children."

Numbers 14:18

CHAPTER 1

The last day of Dominik Weiss's life started out a lot like any other. After showering, he sat down at the kitchen table, drank three cups of green tea, and ate two slices of whole wheat toast—one with honey, the other with strawberry jam. Then he put on a suit, tied his tie, and drove his dark-blue Peugeot to the office.

He was at his desk by eight on the dot. His job at Capital Security was to follow the Asian stock exchanges, which were ahead of the European ones. He shifted company and customer money around based on his analyses. Maximizing returns was his number-one responsibility.

At exactly noon, he took his lunch break in the cafeteria on the ground floor of the office building—alone, as always. He'd been working at Capital Security for more than fifteen years already; his work life followed a disciplined routine. Dominik Weiss was content; he saw no reason to change a thing.

At four thirty p.m., he cleared off his desk and switched off his computer. Most of his coworkers had left early that Friday; he said good-bye to those who remained and wished them a good weekend, a formulaic utterance that required no thought. As was the case with most of his colleagues, the hollow greetings and farewells were automatic.

He got his Peugeot out of the underground parking garage and drove home to Pankow, the district in Northeast Berlin where he and his wife had a two-and-a-half-bedroom apartment.

In one respect, today actually had been different from the hundreds of workdays before it: that morning, he'd awoken in their marital bed alone. And she would not be at home now, he remembered as he jockeyed his car into a parking space. He'd have to take care of dinner on his own. And later, he'd be watching their Friday-night detective shows by himself.

The prospect left him feeling anything but pleased. He already regretted allowing his wife to take this "wellness weekend." She had said she needed a little R & R. The words echoed in his mind. She needed some time for herself. She'd nagged him about it for over a week, talked about nothing else, begged and pleaded, bitched and moaned, until she'd finally worn him down.

As soon as the "all right" had slipped out of his mouth, he'd wished he could take it back. But the last vestiges of respect he still had for his wife, even after all these years, had kept him from driving the unmistakable joy from Annika's face.

And now she and her two friends Kathrin and Helene were off to a health resort in the town of Waren. They'd left the previous afternoon in order to reach the hotel before dark. She hadn't told her husband it was going to be a long weekend—a Thursday-to-Monday affair—until he'd agreed to it.

Well, he thought, *it's not like I need a woman, much less depend on one. And Annika won't get any dumb ideas with two friends along.*

With that, he turned the key in the lock of the apartment door . . . and blinked in surprise. There was no doubt in his mind that he'd locked up when he'd left the apartment that morning. He'd turned the key in the lock twice; he was sure of it. But now, he had only to give the key a quarter turn to the right and the door snapped open. Maybe his wife was back early?

"Annika?" he called out into the hallway. He listened for a reply, but none came.

Loosening the knot on his tie, he stepped inside. He hung his jacket on the coatrack.

"Annika?" he repeated, although he was sure his voice had carried perfectly well the first time.

The kitchen looked exactly as he'd left it that morning. Perhaps he was mistaken; maybe he just imagined he'd locked the apartment door that morning. He grabbed a glass and a bottle of soda and went into the living room. Sitting on the sofa, he filled his glass and took a sizeable gulp. Even though everything seemed normal, an uneasy feeling began to creep over him.

Was that a noise?

Something wasn't right. He sat completely still, thought he heard a faint squeaking sound. The blinds in the bedroom made that sound. He put down his glass and stood up. When he reached the hallway, he saw that the door to the bedroom was ajar. Light shone through the crack, artificial light. The sight alarmed him. He hadn't noticed the light when he'd first walked into the apartment. And it wasn't dark outside. There was no reason for a lamp to be on.

Annika's wasting electricity again, he thought as he stepped inside. Then he jumped. A woman was standing on the other side of their bed, a woman about half a head shorter than he was. She was wearing a black business suit and—a black leather mask. There was a black glove on her left hand; her other hand was hidden behind her back.

The window blinds were down, and the lamps on the nightstands had been dimmed, bathing the room in a pale light.

"Annika? Is that you?"

He squinted. Figure-wise, it could be her. He didn't recognize the suit, but he sure knew the black leather mask. He'd bought it himself, about a year ago, at a sex shop near Schönhauser Allee. A riding crop lay across the bed. Next to it was a pair of handcuffs. He'd purchased those himself as well. But this was the first time that his wife had retrieved the accessories from the back corner of his closet of her own accord.

"Got yourself some new clothes?" he asked. He wanted to provoke a response, wanted to hear her voice so he could be sure that it was his wife.

The woman stared at him through the eyeholes of the mask.

Compliments didn't come easy to him, and he hardly ever paid them. But maybe his wife would react to them. "They look fantastic on you."

The woman only stood there, watching him.

"So much for your wellness retreat, hmm? I told you that you three gossipmongers would be lucky to even make it to the Mecklenburg Lake District without having a falling-out." Already his annoyance was giving way to arousal. "I had no idea you could tie the mask behind your head on your own." He took a step forward. "I guess you'd call that proactive obedience."

He regarded the woman once more. "Oh, so the checking account had enough in it to cover new shoes, too? They look great with the suit. Why haven't you ever bought yourself anything like this before?" His heart began to race. The scene was turning him on.

Last weekend, his wife had donned the mask—against her will. He'd knelt on her back as she lay on her stomach on the bed, spread-eagle, ankles and wrists tied to the four corners of the bed frame. This had been preceded by no small amount of brutality—raw violence, blows with his open palm as well as his fist.

Her resistance had only heightened his arousal. Tied up and pressed against the bedsheet like that, she could only flounder helplessly as he'd used the riding crop to teach her to be silent. When she'd finally shut up, he'd put the mask on over her head and tied it tightly. It had taken a lot of willpower not to let himself finish early.

Then he'd penetrated her again and again throughout the afternoon and evening, taking breaks in between. Degrading his wife to an inanimate object. Just the way he liked it. The only reaction she'd dared show had been the tears dampening the floral pillowcase.

Today, however, he saw neither worry nor fear in her eyes, only cold determination. "Okay then. We'll switch sides for a change. I didn't think you had it in you."

The woman raised her left arm and pointed at Dominik's fly.

"What?" he asked, perplexed. "What do you mean?"

"Take them off."

He started. "Annika? Are you disguising your voice?"

"Off!" The woman repeated in a louder, more forceful tone.

His wife had never spoken to him that way.

"Yeah, okay, fine." He unbuckled his belt and unzipped his fly. Then he pulled his pants down to his calves.

"Shoes."

Dominik untied his shoes and slipped them off. Then he pulled off his socks, nearly losing his balance in the process, and slid his pants over his feet. Now he was down to a button-down shirt and briefs. The briefs were already beginning to bulge.

"Shirt."

Hastily he unbuttoned it, pulled it off over his head, and let it fall to the floor next to the pants.

"Briefs."

He obeyed that command as well, and now stood naked before her. Slowly she brought up her right arm.

Did she find the new whip in the clos—? he wondered, but shrank back before he could finish the thought. The woman was pointing a pistol at him, a pistol with a silencer on the end.

"What the hell? Is that thing real?"

The weapon was pointed straight at his chest, but then he watched it glide slowly downward. His excitement faded. "You think you can frighten me with that toy gun? Nice try!"

But it was too late—the fear was there.

The eyes, something wasn't right about her eyes. Weren't his wife's eyes darker?

Dominik heard a click as the woman released the safety catch. Angry indignation rose up in him. What the hell did she think she was doing? She had no right to scare him like this!

"Annika, cut this shit out. I'm only warning you once. You're going to seriously regret this little show. When I get my hands on you, last week is going to seem like paradise by comparison."

Resolutely he took a step forward.

He saw her finger twitch, and then felt a searing burst of pain rip through him. He thought his abdomen was exploding. Tears came to his eyes. Horrified, he looked down at his body and saw that there was now only a mess of flesh and blood where his penis and testicles should have been. The pain! Never in his life had he felt such excruciating pain.

He cried out. When he looked up again, the woman was standing directly in front of him, her eyes staring resolutely into his. She laid her free hand on his shoulder. The pressure was more than he could bear, and he sank to his knees.

Through his agony, he felt the cold silencer against his temple.

Then everything went black.

And thus ended the last day of Dominik Weiss's life.

CHAPTER 2

Private Detective Sabrina Lampe was dreaming. She was lying in a coffin. She could hear bells ringing. Were those church bells inviting mourners inside for her funeral? .

But she was still alive. She desperately needed to get someone's attention, to pound against the coffin lid, but her body refused to obey her commands. It just lay there, in rigor mortis. Her spirit, meanwhile, detached itself and floated up out of the coffin to observe the proceedings. She knew the room. It was in the funeral home near her apartment, Heavenly Peace. *Nomen est omen.*

In her mind she still called the funeral director Herman Munster, even though she'd learned his real name a long time ago. The dad from the TV show *The Munsters* had sprung to mind the first time she'd met him. She told herself she was using the nickname in a positive sense since the original Herman had been a likable guy. So was her Herman. He'd invited her out for coffee a few times now. After the last time, he'd shown her his selection of coffins.

How romantic, Sabrina. You know what? You're half-awake.

She saw Herman coming toward her coffin. Suddenly he was holding a hammer and began nailing down the coffin lid, pounding one nail after another in quick succession.

No, please don't, I'm still alive!

Sabrina woke with a start. There were no church bells ringing, no one was hammering. Instead, someone was ringing her apartment doorbell like crazy and pounding on the door vehemently as well.

Orientation, Sabrina. You're in your bedroom, lying in your own bed.

She stood up, slipped into her house shoes, and walked to the front door, shaking her head to clear it. *Just switch off the noise, quiet things down.*

When she opened the door, she wished Herman Munster were standing there. Or his literary inspiration, Frankenstein's monster. Because what awaited her outside was far worse: her neighbor, Angelika Hasselmann, looking as if she had pressing business to discuss.

Sabrina stood before her in a thin nightshirt. Good thing she'd actually put one on before going to bed. Even so, she felt small and outmatched.

"Dog crap," said Hasselmann in greeting. Sabrina had no idea what she meant. She'd been in dreamland until a minute ago, and so far, reality didn't seem a lot more believable. "Dog crap," the neighbor repeated.

What does she want me to say? For a moment she considered responding in kind: "Sabrina. Pleased to meet you." But she kept the retort to herself. Mrs. Hasselmann raised an admonishing index finger, then pointed to the floor. Someone had apparently stepped in dog shit before entering the building. The trail ended at Sabrina's apartment door.

Bastion of helpfulness that she was, Angelika Hasselmann advised Sabrina of the unfortunate situation in her incomparably charming way: "This is unacceptable, Ms. Lampe. I'm sure it was your daughter or her skinny boyfriend. He's been traipsing in and out all the time lately. I mean, if that were my daughter . . ." Her gaze wandered down Sabrina's body. "Oh, so it was actually you."

Sabrina looked down. And so it was; it was stuck to her slippers as well. She gagged as the stench hit her nose. That stuff hadn't been there before, when she'd put them on, had it?

"Then you need to set a good example for Laura and clean it up yourself," Mrs. Hasselmann continued. "Otherwise children don't learn properly."

Lara, not Laura! Sabrina corrected her mentally, then turned around and discovered that the tracks led up to the living room door.

"What is that racket? A chainsaw?" the older woman asked.

Now Sabrina heard it as well; it was coming from the direction in which the disgusting trail led. Unlike her neighbor, Sabrina recognized it right away: snoring. And she knew whose it was, too. Neither Lara's nor her boyfriend, Mojito's.

Sabrina was appalled. "I'll take care of it," she exclaimed and shut the door in Mrs. Hasselmann's face.

Not wanting to spread the mess around any more, she took her house shoes off and carried them in as she walked to the living room door, taking care not to step in the brown patches. When she opened the door, her suspicions were confirmed: Carsten Lampe, her ex, was lying on the sofa. A stench of sweat and alcohol hit her. It didn't seem to bother Mielke, Lara's fat red tomcat. He was slumbering peacefully on Carsten's stomach, floating down with each exhalation and then back up with each subsequent snore. He didn't even open his eyes when Sabrina entered the room.

What the hell was Carsten doing here? Sabrina was indignant. And more importantly, who'd let him in? He hadn't had a key for years. Lara had let him in, no question. *Just you wait, young lady.*

Sabrina padded over to Lara's door and opened it carefully. Lara looked angelic lying there, blonde hair framing her lovely young face. Unlike her father, she was a quiet sleeper.

Sabrina held the slipper under her nose. A moment later, Lara's face started to twitch. Suddenly her eyes snapped open, and she stared at

Sabrina in horror. Hastily Sabrina pulled the slipper back before Lara could make contact with it.

Lara grimaced. "What now, Mom? When are you going to let me put a lock on my door already?"

"A lock? When you just let everybody in anyway?"

"What do you mean?"

"Go look in the living room."

"Oh, that." Lara closed her eyes, and Sabrina began to suspect she might have fallen back asleep. She started moving the slipper closer again, but then Lara's eyes reopened. "How did that get on there? And why are you bringing it into my room? Gross."

"Your *visitor* brought it in with him. I stepped in it here in the apartment. Anyway, I'm asking the questions here. What is he doing in our living room?"

"Dad?"

"Of course. Or did you hide someone else in there, too?"

"I think he couldn't remember how to get home."

"You think?"

"He wasn't expressing himself very clearly last night."

"I can imagine. But why would you just let him in like that? Without asking me?"

"You were already asleep. I didn't want to wake you. And Dad said you would throw him out."

"He was right."

"Oh, Mom, he's really not doing well. He was crying."

Yeah, thought Sabrina, *more of his ploys for sympathy. I bought them for way too long.*

"What was I supposed to do? He could hardly stand up anymore. So I brought him into the living room. What's your problem with Dad sleeping here?"

"What's my problem? This!" She held the slipper out to Lara again.

"That can happen to anybody, even if they're sober. Can't I go back to sleep, Mom? I'm super tired."

"Oh, yeah? So now I get to clean up after your father and shoo him out of the apartment?"

"I can help you once I've had a good night's rest."

Sabrina couldn't believe it: her daughter simply rolled over and drifted off again. Should she pull the covers off her? Or dump a bucket of ice water over her head?

"Sorry," she heard a voice mumble behind her. "My fault." Carsten was standing in the doorframe, rubbing his temples. "You got an aspirin or anything?"

"Well, at least your immune system is still working."

As Carsten massaged his head, Mielke rubbed up against his legs, meowing for breakfast. Sabrina pushed her way past her ex and deposited her slipper into his free hand. "Once you've cleaned up the trail you left last night, I'll make you some coffee. And I'll have aspirin for you then, too."

"Oh, did I do that?"

"Yep." She walked over to the kitchen. Mielke followed.

Ten minutes later, Carsten joined them. "All clean," he told Sabrina, who had already sat down for breakfast. "Shoes included." He reached for the aspirin and the glass of water Sabrina had set out for him.

"And the stairs?" she asked.

"Um . . . no, not yet."

"I don't want Mrs. Hasselmann ringing my doorbell every half hour."

"I'll take care of it. Just let me have a coffee real quick, okay?" He sat down beside her without waiting for a reply. "I came here for a reason."

"You couldn't find your way home."

"That's not what I mean."

Whenever Carsten came near her, Sabrina got scared. Scared that she would succumb to his charm again. She knew perfectly well why she'd fallen for him, once upon a time. And even all the years of alcoholic excess hadn't completely killed his charisma. A glimmer of it still shone through when he smiled. She felt a stirring of what she'd felt back then. *You have to get away from him, Sabrina. He's no good for you. You decided you wanted him out of your life years ago.*

"I know you're not coming back to me, Sabrina. I accepted it long ago. Even though it hurts like nothing else. It was my own fault, I know that."

He's not going to play the sympathy card now, is he? Maybe it works on Lara, but not on me.

"No, that's not why I'm here."

"Why then?" *Make him get to the point already. Then make him clean the stairwell, and then good-bye. Ideally, before Lara wakes up again.*

"A friend of mine is in trouble."

A friend? Sabrina knew exactly what kinds of friends Carsten had these days.

"Well, it's more of a drinking buddy," he added, as though having read Sabrina's mind.

"What's his problem?"

"Stalking. Apparently some woman's been following him around constantly."

"And you're sure it's not just delirium tremens?"

"Sabrina!" He sounded genuinely offended by the remark.

"Sorry."

"It really seemed to me that he felt he was in danger."

"So why doesn't he go to the police?"

"It's not that easy."

"Come on, don't make me pry each detail out of you."

"He was in prison for a few years, so he's not a big fan of our justice system."

"Why was he in prison?"

"I dunno."

Sabrina wasn't sure if Carsten was telling the truth.

"Anyway, he's out on parole."

"What does that have to do with anything?"

"He's afraid either the woman or the police want to pin something on him."

"Why would they do that?"

"Don't you want to talk to him yourself?"

Sabrina thought about it.

"I already gave him your phone number."

Well, great.

"He'll be calling you sometime today."

Probably when he's slept off the booze.

"His name is Gerd Lucke. And don't worry. He's got money. He can pay you."

Looks like you're not getting out of this one, Sabrina. "Okay."

"Thanks. Can I have another aspirin?"

CHAPTER 3

"From the looks of it, we've got a ritual murder on our hands." Detective Niklas Steg hung up the phone and closed the notebook he'd been taking notes in.

"We've got something?" Jasmin Ibscher looked at him with wide eyes.

"Looks like it, Jasmin."

"A ritual murder? I thought those only happened on TV."

Nik knew what she was getting at. Unlike him, Jasmin loved the American detective shows currently flooding German television and seemed to spend a lot of evenings watching them. Out of curiosity, he'd checked them all out at some point—quick edits, snappy dialogue, split screen, overly cool main characters—but he'd never managed to watch more than ten minutes of any episode. The cases just had too little basis in reality, too little to do with everyday detective work.

But after what he'd just heard on the phone, he found himself starting to question that assessment. The officer on the other end of the line had described a crime scene tailor-made for the stylish investigators from Las Vegas, Miami, or New York. But the crime in question hadn't been committed over there, on the other side of the pond. It had happened in Berlin, in the Pankow neighborhood.

"Sector 13," said Nik, rising to his feet. "Officers already on the scene."

Jasmin stood and grabbed the car keys on her desk, running the fingers of her other hand through her dark-brown hair as she did so. The two detectives left the State Office of Criminal Investigation and headed north in an unmarked vehicle. The sun was setting over Berlin; streetlights were coming on. "Friday, late afternoon," Jasmin said, concentrating on the traffic around her. "Who picks a time like that to commit a violent crime?"

"You think the perpetrator should have let the victim have one last weekend?"

"No, I was thinking about how I'd been hoping it was going to be a quiet weekend, since I have to spend it on duty."

"From the description of the scene, I doubt we're going to get bored in the next few days. Hopefully you haven't eaten much today."

"So far I haven't gotten the impression that I'm a lot more sensitive than you are."

That was true. It surprised Nik again and again how much his partner could take. He himself always took to heart the things he saw on the job. Most nights he had a hard time switching off after work. Once upon a time, he'd always talked things over with his wife, Hanna. That had been back in Munich, in a home that was no longer his. When Hanna had cheated on him with a coworker, he'd left her and his daughter, Tamara, and the home they'd shared. He'd moved back to his parents' house in Berlin and started providing the care they needed to continue living in their own home, rather than moving to an assisted-living facility. Nik felt terrible about being apart from his daughter, though. He missed her every day.

His mother, Elisabeth, had dementia, and recently her condition had taken a turn for the worse. His father, Karl, was gradually recovering from a stroke and getting his life back together. Before retirement, Karl had worked for the police department as well, and Nik had taken to discussing his current cases with him in the evenings. The way he'd done with Hanna before they'd split up.

Nik looked out the window. He started thinking about the crime, unable to suppress the images it brought to mind any longer. As Jasmin steered the vehicle across the Mühlendamm Bridge spanning the Spree River, Nik took up the conversation again. "The body is severely mutilated," he said.

"Female?" asked Jasmin after a brief pause.

"Male." Nik fumbled at the knot of his tie, searching for words. "At least, he was male before."

"What do you mean?"

"He was shot in the genitals." His gaze remained focused on the Berlin streets rushing past. He heard Jasmin swallow. "I think we're going to need nerves of steel when we get there."

The roads were relatively quiet at this time of day, now that rush hour was over. "Two units are already there. The forensics people are on their way." Nik flinched as the car hit a pothole. "Apparently one guy threw up at the sight."

"Shit."

They reached the crime scene in Pankow a few minutes later. Two police cars were double-parked in front of the building entrance. Nik recognized the silver Ford on the other side of the road; it belonged to Andrea Link, the head of the forensics team.

A small crowd had already formed near the front door. A uniformed officer stood at the entrance to the stairwell, his arms raised in a placating gesture as he called for calm. People hectored him for information.

Jasmin parked behind the police vehicles, and she and Nik walked toward the entrance.

". . . just want to know what's going on . . ."

". . . the police doing here?"

"... stepmother lives in the building ..."

Nik pushed his way past the agitated onlookers. The policeman already had his palm outstretched to hold him back, but then recognized the badge Nik was holding out to him and stepped aside to let the two detectives through.

The stairwell muted the outside noise.

"Watch out!" a female voice barked at them as soon as they entered. Nik stopped in his tracks, and Jasmin bumped into him from behind. Another uniformed officer was sitting on the bottom step, his face white as chalk. He was staring straight ahead, a stunned expression on his face.

Shock, Nik diagnosed.

An older woman had taken a seat next to the officer. She had a caring arm around his shoulder and was holding a bright-red plastic bucket in her other hand. She'd been the one who'd just spoken—Nik could see that in her eyes, which drifted down his legs and focused on the floor just in front of his shoes.

Nik followed her gaze. The yellowish puddle spreading out near his feet contained small pieces of light meat, along with undefinable dark-green chunks. Now the smell hit him as well. The woman had warned him just in time. He nodded at her in thanks before taking a large step over the puddle, Jasmin right behind him, and squeezing past the two seated figures. An officer in white overalls came out to meet them one flight up. The door beside her was wide open.

"Weiss," Nik read on the nameplate beside the door. He showed the officer his badge, and she handed them overalls. Nik and Jasmin tugged them on and donned protective shoe covers and hairnets before stepping inside.

Every door leading off the apartment hallway was open; the lights were on in every room. But he only heard sound and voices coming from one. He walked purposefully toward it.

The grisly scene that confronted him stopped Nik in his tracks. The corpse was lying on the ground—one knee bent, the pelvic area a shapeless, tattered mass of flesh and blood. The head was tilted to the side, lying in a pool of its own blood, a bullet wound in the temple.

Andrea Link was bent over the body, recording her impressions into a digital voice recorder. Next to her, a policeman—in a white protective suit, like everyone else—was taking notes. A third officer nodded at the detective when he saw him. Nik had met him on an earlier case and remembered his name: Arno Manstein.

Everything around the body was soaked in blood; the fact that the carpet had once been patterned beige was only evident near the edges. The killer had apparently walked through the pool of blood without giving it a second thought, because there were several footprints leading to and from the corpse. Most of them led toward the marital bed. When Nik looked up, he discovered footprints on the bed as well—along with a leather mask, a riding crop, and a pair of handcuffs.

Nik saw immediately why the perpetrator had been on the bed: from the looks of it, the killer had walked back and forth several times between the dead man and the wall at the head of the bed to dip his or her fingers in blood, then wipe them on the textured white wallpaper. Although the letters were smeared and uneven, Nik had no trouble making out the message. His lips formed the words silently as he read them on the wall: REAP THE STORM.

"Somebody put in a lot of work on that," he heard Andrea Link say, and he turned toward her. "She must have had to climb up there a dozen times to leave her signature."

"She?"

"Yep. Look at the prints, Nik. I'm pretty sure those are women's shoes."

Nik walked into the room, regarded the relatively small heel on a particularly clear footprint. "You're right. Highly unlikely those were made by a man."

Andrea stood and regarded the wall briefly. Then she spoke into her recorder: "She used the index and middle fingers of her right hand to write."

Nik realized, to his slight bafflement, that Andrea was chewing gum. Apparently, at least one person's stomach wasn't affected by the scene.

She turned back to Nik. "My first impression is that first she blew off the victim's balls, and then she blew out his brains."

Nik didn't care for her choice of words but decided not to comment. "Has anything been changed here?" he asked the officers present, as a matter of routine.

"No," Arno Manstein replied. "Everything's just the way we found it."

"Good."

"We've got enough fingerprints," Andrea remarked. "And I'm sure we'll be able to secure enough DNA material as well."

"So the perpetrator is assuming that we don't have her on file." It was the first time Jasmin had spoken.

"Or else she doesn't care whether she's identified," added Nik. "Who notified the police?"

"A Mrs. Kroger," Manstein said. "Neighbor lady."

"She heard the shots?"

"No, somebody rang her doorbell. When she opened the door, nobody was there. But she found the door to the neighbors' place"— Manstein gestured with his head in the direction of the body—"wide open."

"Where is she now?"

"Officer Hammermüller is taking care of her. You must have seen the two of them when you came in."

In less ghastly circumstances, Nik would have laughed at Manstein's interpretation of who was taking care of whom. "Then we'll go talk to Mrs. Kroger."

After exiting the crime scene, he and Jasmin removed their overalls and went down the stairs.

"You found the victim, Mrs. Kroger?"

"The door was open, so I just went in." She paused before going on. "Usually I would never do anything like that. I mind my own business. But when the doorbell rings and nobody's outside—and the neighbors' door's all the way open like that—I figured something wasn't right."

"Someone rang your doorbell?"

"And how! Pressed the button and held it. My ears aren't what they used to be, so I've got the doorbell volume turned up high. 'I'm coming!' I shouted, but the ringing still didn't let up."

"Strange."

"Probably just some silly children's prank."

"Does that happen a lot?" Nik asked.

"Actually, no. Mostly just older folks here in the building. Only the Voigts have children, but they're still in strollers. It couldn't have been them."

"And then you just walked into your neighbor's apartment?"

"Yes. Was that wrong of me?"

"No, no. Don't worry. Did you notice anything unusual in there? I mean, apart from the body, of course. Any noises? Anything different?"

Mrs. Kroger pondered for a moment. "No noises. And I couldn't say whether anything was different. It was my first time in there."

"How long have you been neighbors?"

"More than five years."

"And you'd never been in the apartment?"

"Mr. Weiss was fairly, well, how do I put it? Withdrawn? Solitary? Peculiar?"

"'Was?'"

"Isn't that Mr. Weiss on the bedroom floor?"

"That hasn't been determined for sure yet. What do you think?"

"Stature looks about right. It never even crossed my mind that it could be anyone besides Mr. Weiss."

"The bed in the bedroom is a double. I assume there's also a Mrs. Weiss?"

"Oh, yes. Lovely woman. But very quiet, almost shy. Doesn't seem too happy."

"Does she work? When does she usually get home?"

Hammermüller retched, and Mrs. Kroger turned back to him for a moment, patting his shoulder as she brought the plastic bucket into position. Then she continued. "No, she doesn't have a job. She takes care of the house. Right now she's away on a trip."

"How do you know that?"

"Well, she told me. Three times, even. Probably thought I'd forgotten. I'm old, but I'm not senile. I do my crossword puzzles every evening."

"Do you know where she went?"

"Waren. In the Mecklenburg Lake District. I went there once with my late husband. Very nice area. Lots of mosquitoes, though. She was headed for some hotel with an English name. Wanted to get massages and pamper herself." The way she emphasized the last part suggested that she suspected it involved something immoral.

"So it's a health resort, a spa?"

"Yes, that's it. But she said there was nothing indecent about it."

A grin flitted across Jasmin's face.

"When was she planning to be back?"

"She said something about a long weekend."

"Do the Weisses have children?"

"No."

"Okay, that's it for now. If necessary, may we ask you some more questions later?" Nik added for the sake of correctness.

"Of course. Poor Mr. Weiss. I'm sure he didn't deserve this. And poor Mrs. Weiss. I can't bear to imagine. Back when my husband—"

Another bout of retching from Hammermüller interrupted the impending anecdote, and Nik and Jasmin quickly excused themselves and went back upstairs.

Through the door on the left-hand side—the one leading to the apartment above the Weisses'—they heard a sonorous voice saying something about Iraq, the German army, and ISIS. Apparently someone in there had the news on at an excruciatingly high volume. Nik pressed the doorbell once, twice, a third time. Then he held the button down. A full minute went by before the door finally opened. An old man stood before them, squinting, with one trembling hand on the doorknob. There was a worn, grimy-looking hearing aid in one of his ears.

"We're from the police," Nik said in a raised voice. The two of them held out their badges.

The man seemed to recognize the emblem at least. "Yes? What is it?"

"Did you notice anything unusual this evening?"

"What do you mean?"

"A loud noise? Maybe a gunshot?"

"Nope."

"Did anyone ring your doorbell?"

"What?" The old man adjusted his hearing aid with the nervous fingers of his right hand.

"I asked if anyone rang your doorbell. I mean, before us."

Now he understood, but he shook his head. "Nope."

"Do you know the Weisses?"

"Who?"

"Mr. and Mrs. Weiss. They live below you."

"I know them."

"When did you last see or speak to them?"

The old man shrugged his shoulders. "Who did you say you were again?"

"Police," Nik repeated and showed his badge once more. At the same time, though, he recognized the futility of continuing. Communication with his mother was similar sometimes. "Thank you for your assistance," he shouted.

The old man nodded and shut the door.

"Next door," said Nik, turning toward the apartment across the hall.

"Voigt," Jasmin read on the nameplate. "The ones with the little kids." She rang the doorbell, but no one answered.

Of the six remaining apartments in the building, only two tenants were at home. Independently of one another, they reported hearing someone ring their doorbells persistently as well. They, too, had assumed it was a children's prank. But apart from that, neither of them had noticed anything unusual—no strange noises, no unfamiliar faces in the stairwell.

Nik and Jasmin returned to the crime scene, where Andrea had just fished the dead man's wallet out of his back pocket and was holding his driver's license in one plastic-gloved hand. "Dominik Weiss," she read out before turning to look at the corpse's face. "He's changed a little, but I think that's him."

Nik's eyes returned to the wall above the head of the double bed. The blood-red script had already burned itself into his mind. Twelve letters, three words. Utterly mystifying. What was the killer trying to tell them?

A chill ran up Nik's spine. He didn't know it yet, but the murderer's blood-scrawled calling card would be keeping him busy for some time to come: REAP THE STORM.

CHAPTER 4

FLASHBACK: THE GERD LUCKE CASE

Gerd Lucke stopped short. The eyes of the woman across from him seemed familiar somehow. He was standing right in the entrance of a discount clothing store, between the security columns that sounded the alarm when someone tried to take unpaid merchandise out of the store. He was carrying a plastic bag containing the pants he had just bought. Special offer. So he hadn't set off any alarm signals, but he froze in that exact spot anyway, because of the woman who entered the store just as he was leaving.

The woman shrank back, then hurriedly averted her eyes and disappeared into the women's department. Long brown hair, subtle makeup, light-blue business suit. No doubt she normally shopped in higher-end stores.

Gerd Lucke shrugged. That happened a lot in life, when people thought they recognized somebody. A smile that reminded them of a childhood friend. A gesture. A wink. The way someone walked.

Probably just a coincidence.

He still believed that when he saw the woman later, at the Alt-Tempelhof subway station. She got out of the car just in front of the one he had been in. She glanced around for a moment, as though getting her bearings, and then their eyes met once more. Hastily she looked away and walked toward the exit. She disappeared behind a panel advertisement for the Berlin State Opera. He shuffled home and forgot all about her.

Two days later, he saw her again. Through his kitchen window. She was standing in the shadow of a kebab stand, watching the entrance of the apartment building he'd been living in for over a year now. If he could just figure out whom those eyes reminded him of. He hid behind the kitchen curtains. She stood there for a quarter of an hour, then looked at her watch and left. Where she went off to, he didn't see—she disappeared from his field of vision too quickly.

The next time he saw her, it was as he was heading to his local haunt, a bar fittingly named the Beer. He needed to blow his nose, and when he pulled his handkerchief out of his pocket, he accidentally drew his keys out as well. They fell to the ground, and when Gerd Lucke bent down to retrieve them, he happened to glance behind himself, off to one side—and there she was, in the middle of the sidewalk, watching him.

That did it. Determinedly he walked toward her. That seemed to scare her to death, and she turned and ran off, nearly colliding with a woman walking her pug dog. Gerd Lucke was over sixty, and he quickly ran out of steam. Pursuing the woman any farther was not an option. What he needed, he decided, was a beer and a shot, so he turned back toward the Beer.

The alcohol helped jog his memory, and he realized who the eyes reminded him of: Marlene, his wife. The same accusing expression. She'd been dead for more than twenty years, and he rarely thought about her anymore. Too much had happened in the meantime. His old, normal life lay far behind him.

Yes, the years in prison had changed him. He kept on drinking, wallowed in self-pity along with all the other patrons. The Beer was always full of people like himself.

When he returned to his apartment late that night, he found a postcard in his mailbox. He had no idea what it meant, and yet it frightened him instantly. The message on it was just three words long: "Sow the wind . . ." And he sensed immediately that the postcard had something to do with both the strange woman and his past.

CHAPTER 5

It didn't matter whether Niklas Steg shut his eyes or stared out the side window into the twilight descending over Brandenburg; the large, bloody letters just wouldn't go away.

On the spur of the moment, he'd decided to inform Dominik Weiss's widow immediately. He remembered a case back in Munich two years earlier where overzealous neighbors had called the murdered woman's husband on his cell phone and told him about the crime. The man had had a nervous breakdown and hadn't been fit for questioning for over a week. But even more importantly, Nik wanted to see Annika Weiss's spontaneous reaction.

A booking confirmation for the Deep-Blue Hotel in Waren had been lying on a desk in the couple's apartment, pointing the detectives to her exact whereabouts. Jasmin Ibscher, who was driving their vehicle down the A24, broke the silence: "I can still see those words in front of me."

"Same here. Any thoughts about what the killer is trying to tell us?"

"It's a biblical reference, isn't it?" Jasmin said. "I haven't had a chance to Google it yet."

"I did. It comes from a verse in the book of Hosea, in the Old Testament. Hold on, I'll read it to you. 'For they have sown the wind, and they shall reap the whirlwind: it hath no stalk; the bud shall yield no meal: if so be it yield, the strangers shall swallow it up.'"

"Sow the wind, reap the storm," Jasmin said. "That's the way I've always heard it."

"Yeah, that's where the saying comes from."

"So that would mean revenge is our motive here."

"Or punishment. That was a proper execution. Our initial theory of a ritual murder doesn't seem very likely to me now." Nik switched to telephone mode and tapped the abbreviation "SOCI," State Office of Criminal Investigation. The officer on duty picked up a few seconds later.

"This is Steg. Have you got anything on the victim yet?"

"Nope."

"No criminal record, arrests, nothing?"

"From a police point of view, he was a model citizen," replied the officer, to Nik's disappointment.

"What about Annika Weiss?"

They had nothing on the widow yet, either.

"Okay, thanks." He hung up and started writing a text. Hi, Dad, he typed. Sorry, I'm not going to make it tonight. Go ahead and eat dinner without me. Love, Nik. Then he stuck the iPhone back into his jacket pocket.

At the Wittstock/Dosse interchange, Jasmin stayed in the lane for the A19.

"Police statistics on murders show a high probability of the partner being the culprit," Nik remarked.

"Yeah, I know."

"And that fits my experiences, too. But the nature of the crime, and the crime scene . . . Hardly a typical murder case. Awfully brutal approach for a woman."

"And why would she take the time to smear those words on the wall?"

"As a deterrent to others?" Nik said.

"A deterrent against what?"

"That's what I'm wondering. Dominik Weiss was being punished for something."

"The apartment seemed nice and tidy. Nothing unusual. Except for the S and M stuff."

"But there must be more to the story. And the perpetrator must have known that Weiss was going to be home alone," Nik said. "Otherwise, it was a weird coincidence."

"Or it really was his own wife."

"If so, she must be truly cold-blooded. But we can't rule out the possibility."

"Maybe we won't even find her in Waren. She drives back to Berlin, executes her husband, smears blood on the wall, and then goes into hiding—or commits suicide somewhere." Jasmin paused for a moment before continuing. "Maybe she's already floating in the canal as we speak—or throwing herself in front of a subway train."

"I doubt this case is going to be quite that simple, Jasmin."

His partner didn't contradict him.

When they reached their exit, they left the interstate behind and took the scenic road that led to Waren, passing between Kölpin Lake and Lake Müritz on their way. The few lights they saw seemed peaceful and romantic. Nik couldn't shake the feeling that the grisly crime clung to him like a virus, as if he were about to infect this idyllic area and violate its sacred stillness.

The newly constructed hotel, pared out of the darkness by the exterior lighting, lived up to its name. The main building was predominately dark blue, with lighter shades for the extensions, window frames, and entrance area. *Perfect color for a spa hotel,* Nik thought. Just looking at the building made him feel more relaxed.

Once the car was parked, he and Jasmin flipped down their sun visors almost simultaneously and looked in the mirror. While Jasmin put on her glasses and checked her appearance, Nik pulled the loosened knot on his tie back into place. He wiped his brow and smoothed his hair to one side, reminding himself as he did so that he was due for his monthly haircut.

They entered the reception area through a revolving glass door. The foyer, too, welcomed the investigators in friendly shades of blue. Even the mustachioed head of reception's uniform matched the interior.

Nik pulled out his badge and introduced himself and Jasmin, then inquired about Annika Weiss. The man said he'd seen Mrs. Weiss and her two travel companions in the hotel wine bar about half an hour before. He showed the detectives the way before turning his attention to a newly arrived couple.

Nik pulled out his phone again. Back in the Weisses' apartment, he'd taken a picture of the wedding photo sitting on a chest of drawers in the living room. He looked it over before showing it to his partner, to jog her memory of the woman's face as well.

Although the wine bar was having a busy night, spotting Mrs. Weiss proved easy. She was a little plumper in the face and had a different haircut, but Nik had no doubt that the woman in the back, sitting on a wooden bench with her back to the wall and raising her glass to the two other women across from her, was the woman in the wedding photo. As he walked in, she glanced toward the wine bar entrance and looked directly into his eyes, with an expression that Nik couldn't read.

He went straight over to the jovial group. "Mrs. Weiss?" he asked to make sure.

She nodded. The two other women regarded him with curiosity.

"Niklas Steg." He introduced himself before nodding in his partner's direction and saying, "Jasmin Ibscher. From the State Office of Criminal Investigation in Berlin."

"Oh, God, did something happen?" Mrs. Weiss set her wine glass down and clapped her hand over her mouth.

"Can we speak to you in private?" Nik gave Annika's two friends a prompting look. They seemed not to understand at first, but then they stood and excused themselves. Nik and Jasmin took their chairs.

"You're going to need to be strong right now," said Jasmin in a soft, gentle voice.

Annika had been staring at Nik up until that point, and only now seemed to register Jasmin's presence. "What happened?" Her gaze shifted back and forth between the two police officers. Her right hand was trembling, and she hastily slid it under the table, as though she'd been caught doing something inappropriate.

"I'm afraid we have some very bad news for you," Jasmin went on. Annika blinked. Nik scrutinized her face carefully.

"It's about your husband, Mrs. Weiss."

Nik was glad Jasmin had taken over the burden of delivering the bad news.

"I'm afraid it is my sad duty to inform you—"

A horribly hackneyed phrase, thought Nik, just as Annika Weiss interrupted his partner.

"Oh, God," she said again. "My husband! What happened to my husband?" Jasmin didn't finish the rest of her sentence, but Annika seemed to read the message from her expression. "He's . . . dead?"

Jasmin nodded. Annika's face went pale, contrasting strangely with her dark nail polish. Her eyes were fixed on an imaginary point on the wall.

"Good evening. Can I bring you anything to drink?" A waiter had approached the table.

"A mineral water, please," said Nik.

"Do you have nonalcoholic beer?" asked Jasmin.

"Of course."

Nik turned back to Mrs. Weiss. She was probably around thirty, and he could see she took care of herself. Taut skin, old-fashioned perm, subtle makeup. Even so, something about her made her seem ten years older. Somehow Nik suspected that her life wasn't a happy one.

Annika picked up her glass with one shaking hand and took a sip. "How—how did it happen?"

"You have our deepest sympathies, Mrs. Weiss." Jasmin took a deep breath. "He was the victim of a crime."

"You mean he was . . ."

Jasmin nodded.

Annika's muscles seemed to slacken. She leaned back. Her gaze wandered to the ceiling.

"Are you all right, Mrs. Weiss?"

Without responding, she turned toward her purse on the bench. After rooting around for a moment, she found the package of tissues she was looking for and pulled one out. She blew her nose loudly, then took a second one and wiped her eyes. The pale pink shadow on her right eyelid was now smeared up across her eyebrow.

"Mrs. Weiss?" Jasmin asked, worried.

"I never thought it would end like this."

"What do you mean?"

"You know. 'Until death do us part.'" A short sob punctuated the last word. "Are you married?"

Jasmin indicated that she wasn't. Nik was silent—Annika's question seemed like it had only been directed at Jasmin.

"You get old together. Your grown children come to visit you, and your grandkids. You walk to the park together, feed the pigeons and the ducks. When the spirit is willing but the flesh gets weak, you can still hold hands and think back on your wonderful life together."

Jasmin let her talk.

"That's how naïve I was about the whole thing. You only get married once in your life, you know? You think long and hard about whether this person's the one. And then you make a decision. For better or for worse. Until death do you part."

When Annika repeated the sentence, Nik's thoughts turned back to the crime scene, to the dead man, the gunshot wound to the genitals, the cold-blooded execution. The abrupt destruction of the couple's future together. And yet Annika Weiss's words sounded scripted to Nik somehow. His gut told him that something wasn't right.

The waiter brought their drinks. While he was there, Annika drained her glass in one gulp and then pointed to it. The waiter refilled her glass from the wine carafe on the table.

"How did it happen?"

For a second, Jasmin seemed to fumble for words. "Your husband was shot in the head." She spared the widow the gory details for the time being. Annika Weiss would learn the exact circumstances of her husband's death soon enough.

"Where did it happen?"

"At your apartment."

"Where exactly?"

"In the bedroom."

"An intruder?"

"We don't know yet."

"But we don't have any valuables. What did he want from us?"

"We've just started our investigation, Mrs. Weiss. Please believe me when I say that we're doing everything we can to find out what happened."

"When did it happen?"

Jasmin told her what time Mrs. Kroger, the neighbor, had called the police.

"Oh, my God. I was at dinner with Kathrin and Helene then. You mean while I was sitting here eating herb-crusted walleye . . ." The idea that her husband had been murdered at that same moment left her speechless. She swallowed, and for an instant, Nik was afraid Annika

Weiss was going to throw up, but instead she reached for her white wine again and washed the shudder down.

Nik had the feeling that she was strong enough to handle a question that he was itching to ask. He spoke up for the first time in the conversation. "Mrs. Weiss, we found a leather mask, a riding crop, and a pair of handcuffs on your bed. Do they belong to you?" It was just a hunch, but Annika Weiss's reaction confirmed that his intuition was on target. She started visibly; her jaw dropped. Vehemently she shook her head, as though denying it to herself. For the first time, Nik felt like he was getting an authentic reaction out of her. It was obvious that she was grasping for words.

"Do they belong to you?" he pressed her, wanting to provoke a spontaneous reaction.

"Yes," said Annika after the moment of shock had passed. "They're ours." Her cheeks reddened as if on cue.

"There's no reason to be ashamed," Jasmin assured Annika to calm her down.

Nik didn't comment.

"Why were those things lying on the bed?" Annika looked incredulous. When neither of the detectives replied, she began explaining further. "You know, those weren't my fantasies. I always found the whole thing sort of—strange. And *strange* is putting it mildly." She lowered her voice. "Perverse, I always said to Dominik. It's perverse." Then she went on in a normal tone: "But what wouldn't you do for the man you love? What wouldn't you do to make your marriage work?"

"We didn't come here to pass judgment about your sex life," said Nik.

Annika Weiss seemed almost disappointed at not receiving validation.

Nik decided to confront the widow with another fact: "Mrs. Weiss, as terrible as it is, your husband wasn't just murdered."

"What do you mean?"

"He was shot point-blank in the genitals first."

"Whaaat?" was Annika's immediate reaction, but it took another second before she actually understood. "How? Why?"

Nik could tell that her mind was racing. "Do you have an explanation for that?" he asked quickly, before she could get herself under control again.

"Me? No. How? He was shot in . . ." She straightened her back; her expression leveled again. Nik could see that the moment of surprise was over—Annika Weiss was back to playing the role she'd rehearsed. He glanced at Jasmin as an indication for her to take over.

"I'm afraid you have a hard road ahead of you," Jasmin said after a short pause. "You'll need to identify your husband."

Annika seemed glad to change the subject. "Should I come with you now?"

"No, no." Nik held up a hand. "There's no hurry. Go ahead and stay here another night. Talk to your friends. That might help."

"You're going to get this guy, right?"

"We'll do what we can."

Annika nodded, and the detectives took their leave. On the way to the bar to pay for their drinks, they passed Kathrin and Helene, whose curious stares intensified. The detectives nodded to them in farewell, whereupon the two girlfriends immediately scurried over to Annika.

"Very interesting," Jasmin said as they left the Deep-Blue. When they reached the car, she moved to unlock the door, but then hesitated. "Hey, Nik, would you mind driving on the way back?"

"Worn out?"

"I don't like driving in the dark."

Nik took the car keys from her, and they got in.

As soon as they were out of the parking lot, Jasmin began analyzing the conversation. "She knew already, didn't she?"

"I think so, too. Did you notice how quickly she gave us her alibi? We didn't say a single word about her being a suspect."

"Something about her reactions seemed rehearsed to me."

"She wiped her eyes, but did you see even one tear?"

Jasmin shook her head.

"And the expression on her face when we walked in," Nik continued. "It was as if she'd been waiting for us to arrive."

They reached the A19 again.

"There were only two moments that didn't seem rehearsed," Jasmin said. "When you talked about the props on the bed, and when you told her about the shot to the genitals."

The fact that Jasmin's impressions lined up with his own reinforced Nik's conviction. "Yeah, she actually *did* seem surprised then."

"Something about this is fishy, Nik, and I don't mean the herb-crusted walleye Mrs. Weiss had for dinner tonight."

Traffic on the highway was light. Nik switched on the cruise control and let his thoughts revisit the blood-soaked crime scene and the widow's reactions.

The sound of even breathing reached his ears. Jasmin was already asleep.

CHAPTER 6

Sabrina had opted to meet the prospective client in her home; it was the least time-consuming option for her. She didn't want to go to Carsten's apartment. Nor to this Gerd Lucke guy's place, either. She didn't trust anyone in Carsten's current circle of friends. Why did Lucke want to hire a private detective anyway? And who knew if the guy would actually be able to pay her? This way, at least, the loss of earnings she feared wouldn't include travel time and expenses as well.

Her office was too small for three people, so she would be meeting her visitors in the living room. She'd chosen a morning appointment, when Lara would still be in school. Otherwise, Sabrina would hardly have been able to send her out of the living room with her dad there.

And she definitely wanted him there. She didn't want to be alone with this Lucke character. Carsten didn't even know why he'd done time.

They arrived together, both wearing white button-down shirts. Gerd Lucke's even seemed like it had been ironed within the past day or two.

She'd pictured someone younger. Carsten had told her Lucke was a little over sixty, but Sabrina didn't believe it—she guessed he was in his midseventies. Nicotine-stained teeth and a swollen red nose seemed indicators of Lucke's moral conduct. A cloud of cologne accompanied the two inside. Apparently, they'd made an effort to mask the other smells, albeit with limited success.

She set a carafe of water on the living room table. Carsten and Gerd Lucke sat down. Mielke appeared on the scene and hopped onto Carsten's lap.

Traitor, Sabrina thought.

Gerd Lucke told her about a woman he'd first seen a couple of days before, at the clothing store. Afterward, she'd followed him.

"Do you have any idea who she might be and why she'd be following you?" Sabrina asked.

"No idea."

"What did she look like?"

Lucke described the woman as thirtyish and attractive, which in Sabrina's view probably meant that she wasn't part of the circles Lucke normally moved in.

"Carsten said you were in jail once."

Lucke nodded.

"Can I ask why?"

"Oh, I left the past behind me a long time ago."

"But it could have something to do with the woman."

"No, I don't think so."

Sabrina's intuition told her that Lucke was hiding something. "If you want me to help you, then you have to tell me everything. The whole truth."

"Just believe me, Ms. Lampe, when I say that the one has absolutely nothing to do with the other."

"He did his time," Carsten broke in. "Maybe we should just leave it at that."

"I can't promise you that I won't need to ask that question again at some point, Mr. Lucke."

Lucke nodded. "Just find out who the woman is."

"I can't monitor you around the clock, though."

"I've seen her in front of my house a few times now. If I go toward her, she takes off. If I wait and do nothing, she just stands there. I'll just let you know when she comes back. I assume you're better in following people than I am."

At, thought Sabrina, *at following,* but she suppressed the urge to correct him. "I have other obligations as well. Surely Carsten has told you that I have fixed hours as a store detective."

"Yeah, I know." He pulled out his wallet. "I'll just give you enough money that it'll be easy for you to drop everything as soon as I call."

Arrogant thing to say, Sabrina thought. *And where did he get the money?*

"I inherited it."

Had he read the question on her face?

"You just turn the tables on her. You follow the woman and figure out who she is and where she lives."

"I hope you're not planning on doing anything stupid."

"No, don't worry. I just want to make her tell me what's going on."

Sabrina looked at the bills peeking out of Lucke's wallet and thought about the trip to Italy she and Lara wanted to take in late summer. Until now, financing the trip had seemed a remote possibility.

"Okay," she said at last. "I'll see what I can do."

Lucke extended his right hand, and they shook on it.

It felt extremely unpleasant.

CHAPTER 7

Ignoring the remaining empty chair, Andrea Link walked right over to Nik, pushed his keyboard and notebook to one side, and sat down on his desk.

Perplexed, Nik regarded the forensicist's dangling legs, which were squeezed into much-too-tight jeans. *Good thing she's not wearing a skirt,* Nik thought.

Jasmin Ibscher came over and handed Andrea a folder of documents.

The two other officers in Nik's office, Emma Dombrowski and Roland Thaler, had already heard a brief summary of the events. Mr. Zimmermann, chief of detectives at SOCI Berlin and Nik's direct supervisor, had assigned the two of them to assist him with the case.

"Would you mind going over what you've found so far, Andrea, so that everyone has heard it?" Nik said.

"Sure thing." Link stopped chewing her gum. "The killer made absolutely no effort to conceal her crime. Starting with the fingerprints. We've got them all over the place. The doorknobs, stuff on the bed, and especially in the bloody letters on the bedroom wall. They don't make it this easy on us very often. Then there's the DNA. There were a few hairs on the leather mask, and we found additional traces all over the room. I managed to connect them to three different people. One, the victim himself. Two, the victim's wife. The third set of DNA is also from a woman, that much we know already. I've run searches in our databases for both the fingerprints and the DNA material—no matches."

"So it's her first crime," concluded Roland Thaler. "Why doesn't she care that she's leaving DNA evidence at the crime scene?"

"She knows that we can't identify her," replied Jasmin.

"Or she didn't even think about it," Emma Dombrowski put in.

"Most likely she just doesn't give a shit," Andrea speculated, "because she's not worried if we link her to the crime."

"Yeah, I don't think she's *interested* in whether we find her DNA at the scene," Nik agreed. "So what about the doorbell prank, Andrea?"

"That was the perpetrator, too. Every buzzer outside the front door of the building has her index fingerprint on it."

"So she left Dominik Weiss's door wide open and then rang every neighbor's doorbell," Nik summarized. "I'd say there's only one conclusion we can draw. She wanted the body to be found." Hearing no disagreement, he went on: "The only question is, why?" Stumped silence from the others. "Let's talk about the murder weapon. You've got something there, too, Andrea?"

"Piece of cake. It's a Makarov." She glanced around at the group before continuing. "Named after its developer, Nikolay Fyodorovich Makarov. It was used in the Red Army from about 1950 onward. For decades, every Soviet soldier, and then every Russian soldier, was carrying one of these handguns around as part of their standard equipment. Even today, some Russian forces still have them."

"What makes you so sure this was a Makarov?" Niklas asked.

"The Makarov uses specially developed and manufactured cartridges— the Makarov nine-by-eighteen millimeter. I found two such projectiles at the scene."

"Is it hard to get a weapon like that?" asked Thaler.

Andrea grinned. "Give me the dough and forty-eight hours, and I'll get you enough Makarovs to equip a whole battalion."

Thaler looked surprised.

"After '45 the Soviets took a bunch of technology with them out of East Germany. After '89 they returned the favor by dumping half their weapons arsenal on the black market."

"Have you checked the ballistics database, Andrea?"

"Did that, too, Nik. No match."

"So the weapon wasn't used to commit any previous crimes."

Still taking notes, as she had been throughout the conversation, Jasmin spoke without looking up: "So we've got DNA and fingerprints, and we've identified the murder weapon. Which is actually a lot of information, except right now it doesn't get us anywhere."

"Let's talk about the motive," Nik said.

"Revenge," Dombrowski declared. "Reap the storm. Sow the wind, reap the storm."

Nik had memorized the scripture: "'For they have sown the wind, and they shall reap the whirlwind: it hath no stalk; the bud shall yield no meal: if so be it yield, the strangers shall swallow it up.' So what wind did Dominik Weiss sow?"

"It must have something to do with sex," said Thaler.

"Of course," agreed Link. "Otherwise she wouldn't have shot his nuts off. She didn't want the guy to reproduce."

A brief silence followed.

"Rape," Jasmin speculated.

"Or a prostitute getting revenge for something," Thaler suggested. "Leather mask, riding crop, handcuffs . . . sounds a lot like a domi- natrix to me." He thumbed through a stack of papers until he found what he was looking for. "It says here that there were no signs of forced entry. Unless the perpetrator had a key, the victim must have let her in himself."

"He ordered in-home dominatrix services?" Emma Dombrowski said.

"It's a possibility."

"We'll check his most recent telephone records," Nik broke in. "And incidentally, some *normal* relationships incorporate those kinds of accessories as well."

"Well, Annika Weiss definitely wore the leather mask at some point, according to my DNA analysis. And there were more than three hundred euros in the victim's wallet. Enough to buy a guy a couple hours of humiliation and spanking."

"And that also rules out the idea that the killer was after money or valuables," Nik pointed out. "But we can't just focus the whole investigation in one direction. Is it possible the crime was committed like this in order to distract us from a different motive?"

"Dominik Weiss worked for a company called Capital Security," said Thaler. "Financial affairs, security services, and personal protection."

The head of forensics nodded. "I know them," she said. "Shady outfit. The CEO's had more than one run-in with the law. Never anything serious, though. Otherwise we'd have shut the place down a long time ago. I'm sure you make a few enemies when you work for Capital Security."

"Would you get us some more information on them, Thaler?"

"Yeah, I'll get on it as soon as we finish here."

"Any other suggestions regarding the motive?" When nobody responded, Nik went on. "Annika Weiss's reaction two nights ago to the news that her husband had been murdered was very peculiar. She acted surprised, but the surprise seemed rehearsed somehow. That's how you see it, too, isn't it, Jasmin?"

"Yeah, it seemed theatrical to me as well."

"And she was very quick to give us her alibi. Normally, when you've just found out your spouse has been killed, an alibi isn't the first thing that comes to mind."

"A contract killer?" Thaler conjectured.

"Women in that field are extremely rare," Nik replied. "But I've been batting around the murder-for-hire idea as well. So that means we need to look for a potential motive for Mrs. Weiss."

The room was silent apart from Andrea busily chewing her gum.

Nik turned to look at her. "You've done fast, effective work, Andrea. It's only been forty-eight hours since the murder. I'm impressed."

"I had good material for the DNA analysis, and I hardly slept," came her brief reply.

Nik searched Andrea Link's face for any signs of sleep deprivation, but found none. "Well then, you should probably go home and get some rest."

"Aye, aye, sir," she said with a salute.

Nik ignored the gesture. "You go out to see Helene Grünmann in Pankow," he instructed Emma Dombrowski. "She's one of the two friends Annika Weiss went to the Mecklenburg Lake District with. The Weisses' apartment is still sealed off, and understandably she doesn't want to go there anyway, so she's been staying with Ms. Grünmann since the three of them returned yesterday evening. Calm her down as much as necessary, and don't let on that we view her as a possible suspect. Just ask her to come down here to the SOCI office with you for more thorough questioning."

With that, Nik turned to Thaler. "I'd like you to summarize for us whatever we've got on Capital Security, and find out about Dominik Weiss's last few telephone conversations."

With a final "That's it for now," he brought the discussion to a close.

CHAPTER 8

The woman Gerd Lucke saw through the peephole of his apartment door was a stranger to him. Her blonde hair skimmed her shoulders; her makeup looked smeared, as though she'd been crying or rubbing her eyes. A brown leather purse in one hand. Late thirties, Lucke guessed. She shifted from one foot to the other, an anxious look in her eyes.

Lucke decided the woman posed no danger, whoever she was, and opened the door. Even though that was exactly what she'd been waiting for him to do, the woman still jumped when he appeared in front of her. "Um, hello, Mr., um, Lucke."

"Yes?"

"I'm visiting the Petrovics, the family living above you."

"Petrovic? Don't know them."

"Like I said, they live above you. I'm a friend of Mrs. Petrovic's."

"Doesn't an unmarried older man live there?" Lucke remembered getting into an argument with him once in the courtyard. He couldn't remember what it had been about. Petrovic kept to himself and rarely spoke. The woman at the door didn't seem like anyone he'd associate with.

"Yeah, exactly, Mr. Petrovic. I'm a friend of his daughter's."

The stranger struck Lucke as odd somehow. And she kept blinking all the time. Another sign of nervousness? "And? What do you want from me?"

"Mr. Petrovic's bathtub overflowed, and I wanted to ask you whether any water's dripping down through your ceiling."

"He's got a bathtub? I only have a shower. There's no way a tub would fit in that rinky-dink little bathroom."

The woman thought for a moment. "Um, the apartment upstairs has the adjacent room as well."

Lucke knew that the units actually were partitioned differently here, in the rear building of the complex. Whereas he had two neighbors on his floor, the large family directly below them had converted all three units on that floor into one big apartment. He couldn't remember for sure what Petrovic's floor was like.

"Hang on, I'll check," he said.

"Great. Thanks."

He left the woman standing at the door and went into the bathroom. The ceiling looked dry.

When he came back into the hallway, the woman was inside his apartment, pointing a pistol with a silencer at him. Her hands were shaking.

Lucke did a double take, berating himself for not listening to the warning voice in his head and shutting the door in her face. "What the hell?" First the stalker, then the weird postcard, and now some strange woman pointing a gun at him. Nothing made sense anymore.

Focusing on the gun, she released the safety with an awkward motion. "Don't move!"

Although she was quite a bit younger than he was, he figured he had the edge strength-wise. But the three steps it would take to reach and overpower her would be more than enough time for her to pull the trigger.

"Please just stay where you are."

She'd actually said "Please." There was no doubt in his mind that this was the first gun the woman had ever held. But he wasn't sure if that made the situation better or worse.

He'd been threatened plenty of times in prison, although never with weapons like this one. Once, somebody had attacked him with a kitchen knife. The crimes he was in for had automatically made him the whipping boy, the lowest rank in the prison hierarchy. He'd had to learn to defuse conflicts whenever he could. "What do you want from me? I never did anything to you."

"Please be quiet. Then this will all go quickly."

Lucke sensed that she was more afraid than he was. "Who are you? Have we met before?" Lucke wondered if she could be one of his former victims.

"I told you to be quiet."

With the way she was trembling, Lucke didn't think this was actually going to go quickly. It was questionable whether she'd even hit him. Not that he wanted to risk it. "I can see that you're not a murderer. Or a burglar. So what do you want from a poor old man?"

That didn't go over well. A contemptuous smile flitted across her face. "You raped your wife."

"What? You must have me confused with someone else. My wife's been dead for more than twenty years."

"I know. But back then, you did. And your daughter."

"How do you know my wife? You can't have been more than a child then."

"And your wife's death was your fault. That's why I'm here."

Lucke wasn't sure whether this woman actually had the guts to pull the trigger. Was it a chance he wanted to take? He had to catch her by surprise somehow. He fell to his knees.

"Please, I'm just a poor old man." He bowed his head. "I didn't kill my wife."

She came nearer. "Maybe not directly, but in a matter of speaking."

Before she could get close enough to place the barrel against his head, he made his move, lunging forward to grab one of her shins in both hands and knock her off balance. Immediately he felt a stabbing pain in his shoulder, but with a surge of adrenaline, he leaped up and punched the staggering woman square in the face.

Her nose made a hideous noise, and blood began pouring out of it. She stared at him for a second in disbelief, then passed out in a heap on the floor. The gun slid out of her hand and skittered across the floor.

Lucke checked his shoulder. Grazed, that was all. He pressed his hand over the wound to stop the bleeding. *What now?* he asked himself. He had no faith in the police. They hadn't even been able to protect him from the other inmates. Even though everything here spoke in his favor—no doubt they'd find some reason to use this against him.

Then he thought of Carsten's wife, the private detective. Maybe she would know the most sensible thing to do. He called her, and she promised to come by right away.

Who is this stranger? Lucke wondered. The purse. Maybe she had something in there that would tell him who she was. And indeed, he discovered an ID card. He didn't think he'd ever heard the name, though. It didn't ring any bells: Annika Weiss.

CHAPTER 9

Francesco Atzori welcomed Nik and Jasmin into his office with a radiant, disarming smile on his face. "I'm delighted to welcome you to Capital Security," he said without a trace of an accent. His black shoulder-length hair was heavily gelled, and Nik thought he saw makeup on the man's face. Atzori offered them coffee and water before inviting them to sit across from him at his desk.

Three oil paintings were hanging on the wall behind the CEO. The one in the middle was of the Colosseum, with the Brandenburg Gate on one side and the Kremlin on the other. Less-than-subtle tributes to the company's business relationships, Nik suspected, because according to his recent research, Capital Security had ties to both the Italian and Russian Mafia. Plenty of suspicions, no proof. Expensive, resourceful lawyers had already helped Atzori box his way out of court several times; he'd never gotten anything worse than fines, which he'd probably paid using petty cash. Straw men had gone to prison in his place. At least, that was how Nik's colleagues saw it, the ones who had worked on the cases in question.

"So you're a new addition to SOCI Berlin?" Atzori asked when Nik introduced himself and Jasmin.

"Started a few weeks ago, yeah." The guy seemed to know his way around the police personnel roster.

"Then I wish you all the best in your new job, Detective Steg." The words actually sounded genuine. "What can I do for you?"

"As we told your secretary, it's about one of your employees, Dominik Weiss."

"A tragedy. Truly appalling." His dismay seemed authentic as well. Either Atzori really was distressed or he was a gifted actor. "I've expressed my condolences to his widow. And we'll continue to provide her with financial support for the time being."

Money sure didn't seem to be an issue for him.

"We've looked at a few glossy brochures, but would you mind telling us again in your own words what your company actually does?"

"Certainly. We have two main areas of business. One, we provide security services—building security and personal protection. Two, we broker financial transactions around the world. The majority of our clients are from Southern and Eastern Europe."

Nik recalled the investigation photos he'd seen of muscle-bound, scar-faced men with Capital Security logos on their bomber jackets. Scary. The jury was probably still out as to whether they were a benefit or a threat, security-wise. He'd also heard about the numerous accusations of money laundering over the years and remembered one racketeering charge that had been dropped after just a few hours. *Something is rotten in the state of Denmark,* Nik had thought when he read the report. His colleagues were just waiting until they finally had enough evidence to shut Atzori down.

"What did Mr. Weiss do for you here?"

"Mr. Weiss worked in accounting."

From out of the corner of his eye, Nik saw Jasmin write the word *accounting* into her notebook and draw a smiley face next to it. "And what exactly did he do in accounting? Post invoices?"

"No, no. Mr. Weiss developed several extremely lucrative financial models for us. He was a master of his trade. Showing kindness to his widow is the least we can do to demonstrate our gratitude."

"What was the nature of these transactions? Could you give us an example?"

"Well, say a businessman came to us from Saint Petersburg because he had some extra money and he considered the investment opportunities in his own country too unattractive or too risky. Mr. Weiss would do research to find out where and how we could invest most effectively on the customer's behalf."

"Businessman," "extra money," and "invest most effectively" had a peculiar ring when Atzori said them. Sounded exactly like the semi-shady types of transactions that had gotten Capital Security dragged into court a few times already. "Did Mr. Weiss take care of that on his own?"

"No, our customer base is much too large for that. We have several specialists like him."

"Is there any way he could have made himself enemies doing this? Other employees that were jealous of his success? Customers who weren't happy with his work?"

"There were never any complaints about him, if that's what you mean. Our customers are generally very grateful."

Nik could certainly believe that.

"And his colleagues respected him."

"Respected" didn't strike Nik as particularly warm.

The banter went back and forth for a while, but it wasn't long before Nik decided that Atzori wasn't going to be of much help. If the murder had anything to do with Weiss's work for Capital Security, he doubted that any potentially useful information would ever cross Atzori's lips. Atzori was as slippery as an eel, untouchable and utterly confident. They would have to get at Capital Security some other way.

In any case, Nik's gut was starting to tell him that the motive for the crime lay elsewhere.

Back in the car, Jasmin said, "I wouldn't mind getting a closer look at that sleazeball."

"A lot of people have said the same thing over the years. He's one tough nut to crack."

"True. I read the files, too. Unbelievable that he's been getting away with it for so long."

"Yep. Clever guy."

"The Jana Matuschek trial tomorrow should go more smoothly anyway."

"The perp is that lowlife Moritz Schütte," Nik recalled. "My second case here in Berlin." He thought back to his first one, the disappearance of Patrick Bender. He'd met a private detective by the name of Sabrina Lampe during the investigation. He would have liked to see her again, but she hadn't responded to any of his texts. A real pity.

Jasmin's voice brought him back to the present. "Must be hard for the victim, something like that. Sitting right across from your rapist in court." As the officers responsible for the case, the two of them had been summoned as witnesses.

"At least this case is clearer. Don't think Schütte's going to see the light of day for a few years now. That'll be a huge relief for Ms. Matuschek."

CHAPTER 10

FLASHBACK: THE JANA MATUSCHEK CASE

The twittering of the birds woke Jana Matuschek. And the pain. She coughed. Everything hurt. Her neck. Her upper arms. Her thighs. Between her legs most of all.

She opened her eyes, which required a huge effort. At first, the bright light swallowed up everything else in her field of vision; then the underside of a bush came into view. There were leaves and small twigs directly in front of her eyes. Jana realized that her head was sitting in the dirt. Something was poking into her chest.

She felt around with trembling hands and discovered that a branch was the source of the pressure. She pulled it away. Baffled, she realized that her breasts were resting naked on the ground. Stones dug into her body and her cheek. When she raised her head, an excruciating pounding began behind her temples. She lowered it again.

Where was she?

About ten feet away, there was a sparrow hopping around. It kept pausing to eye Jana, as though uncertain if she posed a danger. In her present condition, Jana thought, she probably was no match for even the sparrow. There was also an empty bottle of Berliner beer lying nearby. She smelled the forest floor—and roses. Then she fell back asleep.

When she awoke again, the sparrow was gone, but not the pain. She had no idea where she was, much less how she had gotten there. There was something red lying behind the bush, half concealed by leaves and grime. Squinting, she realized it was her top. It looked ripped. Then she remembered her bare breasts. Laboriously, she turned her head to the side and looked down at her body. And so it was; she was lying naked on the ground. Jeans pulled down around her calves. Blood drying on her hips.

Another coughing fit racked her body, and the pounding in her head escalated. Closing her eyes and resting her head on the ground helped ease the pain.

In her mind she heard the sound of ripping cloth. A vague memory arose of rough hands jerking her top apart and tearing it from her body. She moaned. A gentle breeze carrying the scent of roses reached her nose again, adding to her confusion about the situation.

When she opened her eyes again, she noticed distinct grip marks on her right upper arm. Off in the distance, behind the trees and bushes, she saw radiant light, sunlight. Already a good bit above the horizon. It had to be late morning.

Jana burped. It tasted like red wine. She'd gone over to her friend Silvie's, and they'd drunk red wine together. Rioja. She could picture the deep violet label with the white and gold script. San Esteban Rioja 2005. Between the two of them, they'd drained three bottles. And then? What happened after that?

Now she heard noises. Footsteps—slow, even steps and quiet, tapping ones. Someone walking a dog. She wanted to call for help, but she was choked by fear.

What if that was *him*? What if *he* had returned?

He *who?* she asked herself. The guy with the big hands. The one who had torn her top to shreds.

The footsteps faded. Carefully she rotated her head to explore her surroundings. She discovered a park bench nearby, with a narrow path in front of it. On the other side of the path, a rosebush. Antlers.

Antlers? She blinked. Then she saw that they graced the head of a bronze stag. She vaguely recalled where in Berlin she'd seen statues like that, and when she craned her neck a little, she spotted the second one. Behind her, off to one side, she made out a stretch of wire-mesh fence. *The rose garden! I'm in the rose garden in Tiergarten.*

She took a deep breath, as though it would revive her spirits. Then she slowly pushed herself up. A shudder ran through her body—more pain. But she didn't want to give up, didn't want to lie down on the ground again. She gathered up all her strength and sat upright.

Now she could see where the blood on her hips had come from. Her pubic area was full of it. Mixed with soil and grime. With quivering fingers, she felt her pubic hair. Everything was sticky. She swallowed hard and wanted to cry, but no tears came. The bruises on her left arm mirrored the ones on her right, she discovered.

He had pressed her down onto the ground brutally, after *he* had wrapped something around her neck. She reached for her chin, then gingerly traced her fingers down to her throat. She flinched when she touched the raw wound.

Off in the distance, she heard a squeaking sound. A woman was pushing a stroller through the rose garden. She wanted to call out, but only managed a rattling wheeze. The stroller reminded her of her bicycle. She'd been out on her bike the day before, ridden over to Silvie's in the late afternoon. But had she been riding it on the way home as well?

She stood up—and sat back down again. Everything was spinning. It made her nauseous, and she threw up. The pain in her throat got worse. She had no choice but to lie down again.

The sun was high in the sky when Jana regained consciousness. *Sit up!* she told herself. It went better this time. She took a deep breath, gathered her strength, and pushed herself up. A swell of pride went through her as she stood on wobbly legs. Jana bent forward, propping her palms on her knees, and tried to ignore all the pain. Then it occurred to her that she was still naked. She reached for her jeans and pulled them up. The zipper was broken, but the belt was intact and held the pants up.

Cautiously, she attempted to walk. It worked. Bending down to retrieve her top nearly made her black out again. For a moment she shut her eyes and concentrated. Then she grabbed the shirt and straightened up. She spread the top out. The front was torn completely in half. She slipped it on. Maybe if she held the ends together with one hand? Yes, then at least her breasts would be covered.

Her bicycle. If she'd had it with her, it ought to be around here somewhere. Indeed, there was something glinting on the other side of the wire-mesh fence. Chrome. Glancing around to get her bearings, she spotted an exit and made her way around to the other side of the fence. Her bicycle was lying in the undergrowth beneath a bush. She herself would never have thrown it down in there. That must have been *him*. She extricated it from the greenery and set it upright.

But riding it was out of the question. Her sense of balance was playing cruel tricks on her. Still, she was happy to have something to lean on. She grasped the handlebars with one hand, still holding her top together with the other. Her bike moved unevenly as she pushed it—the front wheel was bent, she discovered, and the tire flat.

The first few people she passed on her way through Tiergarten only half registered her presence. But when an older woman stopped to stare at her, she realized how frightful she must look: dirty, bloody, torn clothes, broken bicycle. It didn't occur to her to ask the old woman, or anyone else, for help.

And still the tears didn't come.

Without any concept of time, she exited the dense Tiergarten vegetation near the Austrian embassy, then walked past the Ministry of Defense and approached the canal. She pushed her bike across the Bendler Bridge. From there it was just a few hundred feet to her apartment. As she approached her building, she felt for her key ring in her jeans. She was in luck. The key ring was still there, in the right front pocket, where she always kept it when she went out without a purse.

Then she felt her back pockets. Dammit! Empty. Her wallet was gone. Either lost or stolen. And her cell phone? Had she even had it with her? She'd have to go back *there* and look for her wallet and phone. But first she wanted to go upstairs, into her apartment.

Inside, she started by getting out of the rest of her soiled clothes. Then she got into the shower and just stood there, letting the hot water cascade down. For a few moments, Jana didn't move a muscle. Her mind began to clear.

Suddenly she gasped. *Him!* It was coming back to her. *He* had appeared out of nowhere, had suddenly been standing in front of her. She'd had no choice but to dismount. *He* had tried to talk to her; they'd argued. *He* had prevented her from riding away . . .

And then?

She reached for the shower gel and squeezed some into her right palm. Then she rubbed it into her pubic area until she had worked up a good lather. She ignored the pain. Got rid of all the dirt and blood. The bruises and her thoughts were the only things she couldn't wash away.

Afterward, she dried herself off and wrapped up in her white terrycloth bathrobe. In the kitchen, she filled her coffee machine with water, inserted a filter, and spooned coffee grounds into it.

The police! She had to go to the police and file a report, she suddenly realized. She dressed quickly and took the bus to the station.

At first, the officer on duty looked skeptical when she told him she'd been raped the previous night. But he called a female colleague over, and she led Jana into a small, softly lit room with three cream-colored leather armchairs spaced around a coffee table. Jana sat down. She leaned forward and rested her arms on the table. Before the police-woman asked any questions, she touched Jana's forearm gently.

And Jana's tears finally began to flow.

CHAPTER 11

Sabrina Lampe was torn. On the one hand, she was bored of tracking unfaithful spouses and keeping an eye out for department-store shoplifters. On the other hand, the case she and Nik had first met on two months ago, Patrick Bender's disappearance, had pushed her to her physical and psychological limits. She wasn't sure if she could cope with those kinds of situations all the time. So much suffering, so much blood.

When she arrived at Gerd Lucke's apartment and saw the injured woman lying on the floor, it brought her back to that first case. The woman was doubled up in pain, her face smeared with blood. Sabrina quickly repressed the memory of having suffered through something similar just a few weeks before.

She didn't greet Lucke, who was standing next to the injured woman, only gave him an accusatory look before kneeling down and moving the stranger into a stable position on her side. Then she got some tissues out of her purse and dabbed at the woman's face. Even a layperson could see that her nose was broken.

To Sabrina's relief, the woman was breathing quietly and regularly. "What did you do to her?" she hissed at Lucke.

"Me?"

"Who else? Have you called an ambulance yet?"

"Why?"

"This woman needs help."

"She was holding me at gunpoint!"

At that, Sabrina realized that Lucke was holding a silenced pistol in one hand. "Put that down."

To her surprise, Lucke did as she asked, dropping to one knee before carefully placing the gun at his feet. "I wanted to keep her from running off."

"In her condition?"

"She wanted to kill me."

Sabrina pulled out her cell phone.

"Don't call the police."

Without responding, Sabrina dialed emergency services. A dispatcher picked up almost immediately. Sabrina explained the emergency and gave Lucke's address.

"But I'm innocent. She's the intruder here. She wanted to kill me," he repeated.

"She doesn't look like much of a threat."

"See! This is why I didn't want any cops here. Not even you believe me."

Sabrina sniffed the air. "Have you been drinking?"

"I needed a drink."

"That wasn't very smart." The sound of police sirens was already audible in the distance. "And touching the weapon wasn't too smart, either."

"Dammit!"

Sabrina saw that Lucke was trembling, and she didn't think it was just from the alcohol. He'd been correct in his accusations, she had to admit. She'd been biased against him from the beginning. *Not very fair of you, Sabrina. You should know better.* "Okay, let's just stay calm and start from the top," she said. "What happened here?"

Lucke told her how the strange woman had rung his doorbell on the pretext of overflowing water in the apartment above. And how she had then entered his apartment and pointed the gun at him. If what he said was true, he'd probably be dead now if he hadn't defended himself. Sabrina tried to believe him.

The paramedics arrived and attended to the injured woman, carrying her out on a stretcher moments later.

"You're going to tell the police. You don't have a choice with an incident like this."

"That's exactly what I wanted to avoid. That's why I called you."

"What, did you think I was going to help you dump her somewhere?"

"I don't know. But I don't want to go back to jail. I'm an old man."

"If everything happened the way you say, then why would you have to go to jail?"

"I committed serious crimes, Ms. Lampe. And I've done enough penance for them. But there are a few people out there who don't see it that way. They're just waiting for a chance to pin something on me."

"Maybe now it's time you told me why you were in jail."

Lucke looked down at the ground in embarrassment; his shoulders sagged. "I was a social worker," he whispered. "And I molested some kids."

Sabrina didn't know how to react. Her emotions threatened to spiral out of control. One moment, she was filled with utter loathing; the next, she pitied the miserable wreck standing before her. She thought about her daughter, Lara. More than anything, she wanted to turn around and walk out. The old man just grossed her out. She didn't want to have anything else to do with him.

"Please," he begged her. "I've never gotten back on my feet since then, been in jail a few more times. For other things, petty theft, nothing bad. Last got out a year and a half ago. Since then I haven't done anything wrong. Please, Ms. Lampe." With that, he fell silent.

What was he asking her for? To be treated fairly, at least. "I know someone who works for the police. I'll describe the whole thing to him, honestly and objectively."

Lucke nodded gratefully. That was all he wanted.

Sabrina took her phone out on the spot and dialed the number of the State Office of Criminal Investigation. "May I please speak to Niklas Steg?"

CHAPTER 12

INTERLUDE: *NIGHT TALK,*

101.1 RADIO SPREE ANTENNA

"So that's the weather. It's just after midnight, and you're listening to 101.1, Radio Spree Antenna. And now, *Night Talk* with the She-Wolf."

(Jingle.)

"This is Franziska Lupa, and I hope you're having a wonderful evening. If not, call me. Hello?"

"Yeah, um, good evening."

"Good evening. Franziska Lupa here. Who's this?"

(Silence.)

"You can make up a name if you'd rather remain anonymous."

". . . Veronika."

"Hi, Veronika, you can call me Franziska, okay?"

"Okay."

"I'm really glad you called. What's on your mind?"

"I can't talk to anyone about it. Maybe with my mom, I could have. But she's already dead."

"It's okay, Veronika. I'm listening."

"This feels wrong somehow, like I'm betraying my husband."

"Are you calling because of a disagreement with your husband?"

"No. Yes."

"It's about your husband?"

"Yeah."

"How long have you been married?"

"More than ten years."

"Happily married?"

"Yes. For the most part, yes."

"What do you mean by 'for the most part'?"

"Well, the usual wear and tear from living together for years. Just little things."

"Do you have children?"

"No."

"You don't sound satisfied. Do you wish you did?"

"Yeah."

"Is that the problem, Veronika?"

"No. Yes. That, too."

"So it's related to that?"

"Yeah. I've already had myself checked up, too."

"And?"

"Everything's okay with me physically."

"What about your husband?"

"He refuses. He says that he's perfectly fine and he feels healthy."

"Feeling healthy and being healthy are two different things."

"Yeah, I know."

"Is this something you and he can normally discuss?"

"Hardly ever. He usually brushes me off when I try to bring it up. I have to catch him at a good moment if I want him to listen to me."

"Have you looked into couple's therapy?"

"Yeah, but he doesn't want to do that."

"I can hear that you're crying, Veronika. I'm here with you, I'm listening to you, and I want to help you, okay?"

"Okay."

"There's something else you haven't told me yet. I can feel it."

"The photos."

"Photos?"

"Childhood photos."

"What kind of childhood photos?"

"There aren't any. Everybody has childhood photos, don't they?"

"I don't understand."

"He doesn't have any of himself. I showed him my old photos just after we met. Baby pictures, my first day at school, first communion, my confirmation. And of course I wanted to see some of his, too. He told me they'd all gotten lost when he and his family had moved. All their photo albums, and the negatives, too."

"That's really frustrating. But it can happen."

"That's what I thought as well. And my in-laws confirmed the story."

"And now you don't believe your husband anymore, Veronika?"

"It's not a question of believing. I saw the pictures."

"Oh. Where did you see them? How did you find them?"

"It's really not like I was snooping around in his parents' apartment or anything. I was there to water their flowers while they were on vacation."

"And that's when you discovered the pictures?"

"Yeah, a whole album. It was on the bottom shelf of a bookcase, on the far left-hand side of the wall."

"What did you see in the photos?"

"My husband. His face, no doubt about it. As a child, with other children, at school, on holidays."

"And?"

"He had skirts on in all the pictures. He was a girl."

CHAPTER 13

FLASHBACK: THE JANA MATUSCHEK CASE

"What time's it?" Jana asked, leaning forward. Her tongue felt heavy.

Silvie Kessler, who was sitting across from her on the living room sofa, turned and peered at the digital clock. It took her a few seconds to make out the green digits. "'Bout one," she said.

"Really? So late already?" Part of Jana's brain was aware that she was slurring her words but seemed unable to put a stop to it. "I thought it was like 'leven thirty or somethin'." She picked up her wine glass and leaned back in her armchair.

"Should I open another?" asked Silvie.

"Nah, 'sokay. We killed like three bottles already." The wine bottles on the table looked blurry. Jana concentrated on them until their outlines were back in focus again.

"But you've got tomorrow off, don't you?"

"No," Jana replied, "I just don' hafta go to class. I wanna go to the clothing bazaar at two. Gotta be fit again by then."

Silvie shuddered. "Digging around in old clothes!"

"Most of 'em are washed. And there's people who still need the old stuff."

"Yeah, yeah, I just still don't get why you do that for free."

Jana didn't have the energy to start discussing principles again. "Jus' how it is." She finished her glass and tried to stand, her balance wobbly, and she fell back into the armchair. After a moment, she got up again, slowly, and this time she succeeded. She swayed only slightly; the living room did the same.

"Okay, we've gone through our whole list of friends, I think."

"Yeah, 'nough bitching." Jana grinned.

Silvie dragged herself to her feet, too. Jana reached out to collect the empty Rioja bottles.

"Don' bother," Silvie told her. "I'll clean that up tomorrow. No rush."

"If you say so." Jana fished her key ring out of her pocket.

"You're not gonna ride *now*, are you?"

"Sure. In my condition, my bike knows the way better'n I do."

"I don' think that's such a good idea. Better jus' push it."

They had this miserable conversation every time, much to Jana's irritation. She didn't feel like getting into it tonight, so she pretended to back down. "Yeah, 'sprobably better."

Jana saw Silvie raise her eyebrows. Her friend didn't seem to believe her, but she was probably too tired to say so. "An' don't go through Tiergarten. Take Hofjägerallee. 'Sat least lit up."

"Yes, Mom."

Silvie laughed. "Sorry. Didn' mean it like that."

"'Sokay," Jana said, holding her arms out.

Silvie accepted the invitation, and they hugged warmly.

"Night-night, honey," whispered Jana.

"Get home safe."

They let the hug linger, then kissed each other on the cheek. Jana walked to the apartment door, stumbling over a shoe rack on the way. She expected her friend to comment, but Silvie didn't react. At the stairwell, Jana glanced back one last time. The two of them smiled at each other through the open door, and then Silvie disappeared into her apartment.

The stairwell light went out as she was making her way down. *Damn,* thought Jana, *am I that slow?* The light usually stayed on long enough for her to get down from the fourth floor and exit the building. She felt her way along the wall—and started at a sudden movement. Was there something there? Was that a shadow?

Realizing it was her own, she breathed a sigh of relief and felt for the light switch. She pressed it, and the stairwell lit up again. Now she hurried as best as her condition would allow.

Down in the light of the building entrance, she fumbled with her keys for a while before finally managing to open her bike lock. Although she didn't think Silvie was watching, she pushed her bicycle at first. *Damn,* she thought as she realized she still hadn't gotten the light on her bike fixed. Once the apartment complex was out of sight, defiance and obstinacy won out over common sense: she got on.

Twenty feet was all she managed before she had to hop down and try again. She got a little farther on the next try, but ended up losing her balance again. "Third time's a charm, Jana," she told herself. And then she managed to stay on the saddle, which made her proud. That she was weaving all over the road seemed like an acceptable compromise.

She stopped at a red light on her way out of Silvie's neighborhood; when she started pedaling again, she nearly hit the curb with her front wheel, just barely managing to jerk the handlebars over. She managed to stay upright but veered into the oncoming traffic lane. Luckily, there were no cars anywhere in sight. She saw the Victory Column off in the distance and headed toward it.

Only a few cars had passed her by the time she reached the land-mark, where she had to stop. She was completely out of breath and suddenly dead tired. She made out the blurry letters on a street sign: Hofjägerallee.

Straight through Tiergarten is shorter, she thought. *Why should I take a different route than my usual one?* She crossed the street and pedaled onto the familiar narrow path through the trees of Tiergarten.

The light from the streetlamps illuminated her path for a few moments, but then the darkness began closing in rapidly. The clear night sky provided just enough light for Jana to find her way, but it required all her concentration. Which was why it wasn't until the very last moment that she saw the man jump out from the trees, directly into her path.

She squeezed the brakes with both hands. Feet on the ground, quick. She wobbled, but managed to recover her balance.

Now the man was simply standing in front of her. Dark-blue T-shirt, sweat stains underneath the sleeves.

Was it just her, or was the guy swaying as well?

She turned her front wheel and moved to the right. The man took a corresponding step to the left.

"Hey. What's the big idea? Let me through!"

The guy wasn't grinning, was he? She tried to push the bike around the man in the other direction, but he blocked her path again. "Move aside!"

He didn't move. The corners of his mouth slid upward derisively. "What do we have here?"

"Get lost, dipshit!" Only after she'd said it did she begin to realize what danger she might be in. "I just want to get home, okay?"

"Oh, goin' home, are we . . ."

"I can take a different route."

But as soon as she started to turn her bike around, the man came closer. Now, for the first time, she could see his eyes. They seemed glazed. *This guy's drunk, too,* she thought. *He's weaving.*

She took her right hand off the handlebar and punched the man in the stomach. When he doubled over, she kicked him, and he stumbled backward. For a moment, she had the upper hand. She got back on her bike and started pedaling.

She heard crunching noises on the path behind her. *He's running after me.* She tried to speed up. The crunching sound didn't alter. *He's keeping pace with me. Dammit!*

Now she was moving in a straight line, not weaving at all.

The crunching noise—was it still there? Had he run out of steam after all?

For a moment she thought she was safe—until her escape route ended abruptly at a padlocked, chest-high gate. She jumped off her bicycle, grabbed the top of the metal gate, and pushed. No luck. She pulled, then pushed again. *No way!*

The crunching footsteps behind her grew louder. They sounded calmer now, more even, as though her pursuer was confident of his victory and wasn't bothering to hurry. Jana looked around. Undergrowth to either side. No chance of putting enough distance between herself and *him.* She heaved herself up and over the gate.

Now her pursuer sped up. Then he was there, faster than she'd expected, with only the abandoned bicycle and the gate between them. He leaped over the bike and reached through the iron bars to grab her. She ducked away. He snarled furiously.

For a second, their eyes locked. Like Jana, he seemed to have sobered up a lot. She took off running and heard a muffled thud behind her. No doubt about it. *He,* too, had climbed over and landed on her side of the gate. She only made it ten more meters before he grabbed her shoulder and jerked her back violently.

His viselike grip spun her all the way around, and she lost her footing, landing on her butt. The man stood over her, legs apart. He was winded, breathing heavily, but he managed a grin. She crawled backward. He took a step forward, toying with her.

"What do you want?" she asked.

His grin widened. "Like you don't know."

Without taking his eyes off her, he reached for his belt buckle. Then his eyes narrowed. "We met?"

She didn't reply.

Suddenly he seemed to light up. "Oh, yeah. 'Syou, ain't it?" He unbuckled his leather belt and jerked it out of the loops. "Long time no see. Where ya been? I missed ya."

"I don't know what you're talking about."

The man laughed loudly. "Don' make no difference anyway." Holding one end of the belt in each hand, he bent down. She tried again to back away. With one quick movement, he swung the belt over her head. She let herself fall backward, but it was too late. Smoothly, as though he'd practiced the motion plenty of times, he looped the belt around her neck once more.

Now she began punching and kicking at him. He danced back and forth, dodging her attacks. Then he pulled the ends of the belt tight, cutting off her air. Tears sprang to her eyes; her resistance weakened, providing an opportunity for him to drape the belt in such a way that he could hold it in one hand. Then he loosened his grip a little. "Yeah, fight back. Keep squirmin'. I like that."

The angle he held her at kept her feet from landing any serious blows. He deflected one punch easily with his free hand and spotted another well-aimed jab in time to swivel out of the way so that it only hit his thigh instead of his genitals. Once more he pulled the noose tight, and she was forced into stillness.

He sank down onto her and pulled her arms down to her sides, then pressed his knees onto her forearms. She tried to arch up to free her hands but didn't have a chance. His entire body weight was pinning her down. The belt was tight around her neck. Her head and heart were pounding. With great effort she drew air into her lungs, enough that she wouldn't suffocate, but not enough to give her strength.

Her view of her tormentor grew hazy. She heard a ripping sound and realized he had torn her top off. Next, he raised her hips, tore her jeans open, and jerked them down. With all her remaining strength, she attempted to sit up. Roughly, he grabbed her upper arms and pushed them into the ground.

She knew she had lost. She could already feel his erection on her thigh. He rubbed it against her. Then he slid farther up. She gasped for air and felt his fingers on her throat, digging in between the leather of the belt and her skin. At the same time, he forced himself inside her.

Jana faded into unconsciousness.

CHAPTER 14

Sabrina saw Nik's eyes light up for a moment at the pleasure of seeing her again. As requested, he'd come to Gerd Lucke's apartment by himself. He pressed Sabrina's hand warmly in greeting. When he introduced himself to Lucke, he was more reserved. "So, what's this about?"

Sabrina started from the very beginning. Her ex-husband's request. Her first conversation with Lucke. His call today. Her arrival at his apartment. The woman and her injuries.

Lucke was silent until the moment when Nik asked why he hadn't just called the police immediately. "Better if I tell you right away," he spoke up. "All you'd have to do is put my name into your computer and you'd find out anyway. I have a criminal record. I'm out on parole." He explained the reason for his jail sentence as well, speaking quietly, staring at the ground in shame.

Sabrina could see that Nik was grappling with reactions similar to the ones she'd had upon hearing Lucke's confession. She knew Nik had a daughter of his own—about Lara's age.

"Assault," Nik declared at last.

"In self-defense," Sabrina added. To some degree, she felt she'd sold Lucke out to the police. Now, she realized—with very mixed feelings—she was taking on some responsibility for his fate. But Lucke's gratitude for her intervention was plain to see.

Now Lucke began telling Nik about the other woman as well, the one who'd been stalking him for several days. When he mentioned the postcard he'd found in his mailbox, Nik started in surprise. "Can I see it?"

"I tore it up and threw it out."

"That wasn't very smart. When was that?"

"Last week. Trash is long gone by now."

Nik had Lucke recount the day's events again from his point of view, in precise detail, right up to the ID card he'd found on the woman with the gun.

"Annika Weiss was her name," Lucke recalled.

At that, the muscles in Nik's face twitched. Sabrina could see that he knew the name and that he was surprised to hear it in this context. First, his reaction to the postcard, now to Annika Weiss. Sabrina was beginning to suspect that Lucke and his stalker were pieces in a much bigger puzzle. Her curiosity was piqued.

"I could have you temporarily detained," Nik remarked when Lucke had finished.

Again Sabrina stepped in to protect the old man: "I don't think that will be necessary. I'm sure Mr. Lucke will remain in the city and be available for additional questioning, isn't that right?"

Lucke nodded quickly. "I report to my parole officer every two weeks, without fail. He'll tell you that I haven't gotten into any more trouble and that I'm not a flight risk."

"Okay," said Nik. "I'm taking you on your word, Mr. Lucke."

But Sabrina sensed that the remark was actually directed at her.

"Can I give you a ride anywhere, Ms. Lampe?"

"Oh, I drove here myself. But I'll come downstairs with you."

Sabrina noticed that she felt good in Nik's presence—just like last time, when he'd picked her up from the hospital. She was glad to see him again, albeit in less-than-ideal circumstances.

They walked down the steps in silence.

Only once they were outside, in front of the door to the building, did their eyes meet again. She had to tilt her head back to look at him— he was nearly two heads taller. Nik seemed open and friendly, but there was something reproachful about his expression.

"Something on your mind?" she asked.

"Well, yes, actually." He appeared to wrestle with himself for a moment before finding the courage to speak. "I would have liked to see you again sooner."

Sabrina's heart jumped. "Same here."

"But why didn't you answer any of my texts, then?"

"Texts? What texts?"

"I wrote you three. About a week after you got out of the hospital."

Dammit, she thought, *my old phone! Better not go into detail. How embarrassing.* "Um, I had a little mishap with that phone. I don't have it anymore. So there were a couple of days where I couldn't receive any calls or texts." *So unprofessional, Sabrina. And you call yourself a private detective.*

"But you had my number, too."

"I'd saved it to the phone, too. All gone."

"And the number for the station . . ."

"I didn't have the nerve. I didn't realize you were so serious about it."

"What do you mean, 'so serious'? I just thought it'd be nice to have coffee with you sometime."

You're only making this worse, Sabrina. You're acting like a teenager. Your whole face is probably red. Best just get on your way here. "My car's back there," she said, pointing. "I'm in a no-parking area. I gotta go."

"Well, what do you say?"

"About what?"

"Coffee?"

"Sure, that would be nice. Send me a text, and we'll set something up." She bit down on her lip. "Sorry, I mean my phone is new, but the number's the same."

"Okay, I'll give it another shot."

"I'll write back this time. Promise."

And then she made a beeline to her car before she found any other ways to put her foot in her mouth.

CHAPTER 15
FLASHBACK: THE JANA MATUSCHEK CASE

The woman sitting across from Niklas Steg struck him as exceptionally attractive. Twenty-nine years old, as he'd learned from the criminal complaint she'd filed. They'd brought the homicide division in because they suspected attempted murder. The woman had shoulder-length blonde hair; her makeup was tasteful. Except for her red, swollen eyes, Nik might have pictured her on a magazine cover.

They were seated on cream-colored leather armchairs, a low coffee table between them. The other interrogation rooms were plainer, more businesslike, but this one was set up especially for difficult and sensitive conversations. There was even a vase of colorful flowers on the little table.

Jana Matuschek's eyes wandered nervously around the room. She made eye contact with Nik for just a second and then looked away, lids flickering. She seemed more comfortable talking to Jasmin, so he remained silent and prodded his partner under the table with his foot to indicate that she should be the one to talk. The camera behind Nik whirred quietly. He checked his paperwork to make sure that Jana Matuschek had agreed to the taping.

"This is my colleague, Niklas Steg." Jasmin gestured to him with her head. Nik gave Jana a friendly nod, but she paid him no regard. The scarf around her neck bothered Nik vaguely. It seemed out of place.

"My name is Jasmin Ibscher." Jasmin waited for a moment to make sure that Jana had understood. "We're very sorry to hear what happened to you, Ms. Matuschek."

Jana didn't react.

"The officer you spoke to earlier gave us the preliminary information about . . ." Jasmin hesitated, searching for the most neutral word possible. "About the incident."

Nervously, Jana slid from one side of her chair to the other and back again. She needed psychological care, Nik could see. Good thing she'd filed an official report. Too many women never went to the police, either out of shame or because they were afraid of ending up in the public eye. Or because the rapists had been their own husbands.

"But it would help us considerably," Jasmin continued, "if you would go through it once more and give us the exact sequence of events."

Jana studied the table.

"Ms. Matuschek? Everything okay? Do you need some more water?" Jasmin glanced at the plastic bottle on the table and then at the empty glass in front of Jana.

"No," Jana replied. "That's okay." She collected herself and sat upright. "He came out of nowhere," she blurted out. "Jumped into the road, just like that."

"Can you describe him?"

"About my height. Maybe five seven. Black hair, straight, not styled as far as I recall."

"How long was his hair?"

Jana's eyes darted over to Nik. "About like his. Neck bare."

"How old would you estimate he was?"

"Early thirties."

Nik could tell how agonizing it was for the young woman to have to remember. Unfortunately, it was crucial in an investigation to do so, and the sooner the better. The more recent the memories, the more precise. With every subsequent round of questioning, the likelihood increased of something being forgotten or, in some cases, added in by mistake.

"Can you describe his face?" Jasmin said in a muted voice.

"No. All I can picture is his mouth, the way he smirked at me."

"What did he have on?"

Jana furrowed her brow. "A dark-blue T-shirt. There was a stain of some kind on the chest." She paused. "And sweat marks under the armpits."

"You could see sweat marks even in that dim light?"

"Yeah. You know, those white marks that dried sweat leaves behind. And he was totally drunk. I'm sure about that." She began massaging her temples.

"Headache? Would you like an aspirin?" Jasmin looked at her attentively.

When Jana nodded, Nik stood up and went into the hallway, where he asked a passing officer to bring them some painkillers, and then returned to his seat.

Jana reached unconsciously toward her scarf, hands trembling slightly, and rubbed her neck as though it itched. As she did so, Nik saw obvious strangulation marks slip into view.

"Now, Ms. Matuschek. You said the incident occurred on the sidewalk in the rose garden. But you woke up behind a park bench, correct?"

Jana nodded.

"And you can't remember how you got there?"

"No. My bike wasn't in front of the entrance gate where I'd dropped it, either." After considering for a moment, she added, "I have bruises everywhere. He might have thrown me into the bushes . . . afterward."

There was a knock at the door.

"Come in!" called Nik, and the officer he'd spoken to before brought in a tray with water and two packets of aspirin. He set it on the table and left.

Jana downed the contents of one of the packets, then resumed speaking. "He must have just chucked my bike into the bushes, too."

"This is very important, Ms. Matuschek. Concentrate, please. Think about the man's face again. Do you know him?"

Nik thought he detected a flicker in Jana's eyes, but she shook her head. Then she repeated her answer, as though confirming it to herself: "No, I don't know the man."

"You showered after the incident," Jasmin read from the case file in front of her.

Jana looked at her, expressionless. "The doctor who checked me earlier already told me that was a mistake. I hadn't thought about it."

"What about your clothes?" Jasmin went on. "Did you wash them as well?"

"No."

"Very good. Is it okay if we come with you when we're done talking here and pick up the clothes? We may be able to find DNA material on them. Hair or something."

Jana nodded.

Jasmin took a deep breath, paused for a moment, and then spoke again. "Ms. Matuschek, do you think you would be able to describe the entire incident for us, starting from the moment you left your friend's house?"

Jana drank some more water and took a moment to gather herself, then began another detailed recounting. The more she told them, the more Nik prayed they would find usable evidence on Jana's clothing.

CHAPTER 16

The forensics team had finished all their work in the Weisses' apartment, and the apartment complex was quiet when Nik and Jasmin arrived. Nothing suggested that someone had been brutally murdered there just days before and that the place had been crawling with police and reporters. A call to the hospital had informed the detectives that Annika Weiss had received only outpatient care and returned home.

She opened her door shortly after they rang the bell. A palm-sized bandage covered the middle of her pale face. Her hands shook. When she invited the officers in, her voice was quiet and uncertain.

On the drive over, Nik and Jasmin had discussed the possibility of her being a flight risk. Now, seeing Annika Weiss in this condition, Nik knew they had nothing to worry about. She had definitely been more self-confident a few days before in Waren.

She led them into the dining room, where they seated themselves at the table. Nik declined the coffee she offered him.

"I hadn't expected we'd meet again under such circumstances," Nik said. Annika Weiss was silent. He decided to get straight to the point. "Mrs. Weiss, what's going on here? What did that Lucke guy do to you?"

"Nothing." Her answer was barely audible.

"Then why did you want to kill him?"

No response to that, either.

Now Jasmin tried her luck. "How do you know Mr. Lucke? What's your connection to him?"

Mrs. Weiss lowered her eyes.

Nik again: "Mrs. Weiss, your husband was murdered. And then afterward you show up at somebody's place with a gun in your hand and threaten to kill him. Why?"

"He was a pig," she whispered.

"A pig. Why was he a pig? Why did he deserve to die?"

"He hit me. Again and again."

"Lucke?"

"My husband."

"And that's why you killed him?"

"No. I fantasized about it a thousand times, but I couldn't go through with it."

That much Nik believed.

She looked up, and her expression hardened. "As you know, at the time of his death, I was in a hotel in Waren."

Half a dozen witness statements had confirmed that by now. It couldn't have been her. "But what about Lucke?"

"He's a pig, too."

"I know he molested children years ago, yes. But he went to jail. He finished serving his time years ago."

"Serving his time?" she echoed derisively. "What a justice system. The children suffer for the rest of their lives while that pig gets to go back to living a normal life."

"Mrs. Weiss, were you molested by Lucke as a child?"

She looked alarmed. "No, no, thank the Lord."

"How do you know him?" Jasmin said.

"I don't know him at all."

This wasn't making sense to Nik. "Then how do you know what he did, and that he was in jail?"

More silence.

Suddenly Nik had an idea. "Did someone else hire you to bring Lucke to justice? Someone who killed your husband in exchange while you were in Waren making sure you had an alibi?"

She kept her eyes down as she pondered her response.

"God dammit," snapped Jasmin, pounding her fist on the table. "Talk to us."

Nik flinched as much as Annika Weiss did.

"I think I'd like to get a lawyer." She stood up, signaling the end of the discussion. "I'd prefer if you left."

Perhaps that would be the best course of action for now, Nik thought. He decided to oblige her, and the two detectives left the apartment.

Of course, they had sufficient reason to arrest her, but it would probably be more effective to lull her into a sense of security. She was more useful to them as a free woman.

Annika Weiss wasn't a murderer—someone else was behind this. And Nik had an idea who could help him find out more about Mrs. Weiss.

CHAPTER 17

FLASHBACK: THE JANA MATUSCHEK CASE

Nik clicked on the e-mail he'd just received from his colleague Andrea Link in the forensics department. The header alone had his attention: "Results of DNA Analysis." Before he'd even finished reading the first sentence, he announced, "We've got him."

"Who?" Jasmin asked from her desk. "The rapist?"

"Yeah." Nik didn't look up from the screen.

"That fast? Wow." Only three days had passed since the crime.

"Andrea e-mailed you a copy of the report."

They'd found sufficient usable material on Jana Matuschek's clothing. The exact lab data didn't particularly interest Nik; he was just as mystified by chemical formulas as he had been in school. So he skimmed over those lines. "Database match," the e-mail announced farther down, "99.9 percent certainty." That was the part he cared about.

"Moritz Schütte," Jasmin read aloud when she came to the end of that paragraph.

"Never heard of him."

"Let's see what his record says."

Within seconds, they had his information on the screen. The file photo showed the rounded face of a man around thirty, with short black hair sticking out every which way. The block of text underneath listed the man's personal information and criminal record.

"Theft, blackmail, unlawful possession of a firearm," read Jasmin.

"Long list."

"Attempted rape," Nik noted. "He spent most of the last five years in Tegel Penitentiary."

"With Jana Matuschek it was more than just attempted."

"True, unfortunately."

"Says here that he meets regularly with his parole officer, and he's got a permanent address as well."

"Zip code 13559—that's in Wedding, right?"

"Think so."

Nik printed a color copy of Moritz Schütte's photo and stuck it in an envelope. "We're leaving now." Then he took Jana Matuschek's cell phone and wallet out of a drawer. The forensics team had released them both already.

"You want to stop by Ms. Matuschek's?" Jasmin said.

"Should be pretty much on the way. I'd like to show her the photo before we track down this Schütte guy."

Twenty minutes later, they rang Jana's doorbell.

She invited the two of them inside, seeming despondent, but a good deal more composed than at their last meeting. They sat down around the dining table in the kitchen, declining the tea she offered them, since they didn't want to stay long.

"We found your cell phone and wallet in the rose garden, Ms. Matuschek," Nik said, pushing the items across the table.

Jana checked to see if her phone was still working and seemed satisfied with the results. Then she inspected her wallet.

"Everything there?"

"Yeah, looks like it. Thanks." She tried to rub the dirt and grass stains off the leather, without much success.

Cautiously, Nik pulled the photo out of the envelope and laid it in front of Jana.

"Is that him?" she wanted to know.

"I was about to ask you the same thing," Nik replied.

Jana shook her head. "It all went so fast."

Nik recalled the three bottles of Rioja that Jana had polished off with her friend Silvie on the night of the crime.

"I don't remember."

"Concentrate, Ms. Matuschek. Think about the sweat stains you saw, and then work your way up in your mind. Look him in the face."

Jana spent another thirty seconds staring at the stranger's visage. "No," she said at last, looking helpless. "I don't recognize him. It could be him. The haircut and color are right."

"It's not a big problem," Nik assured her. "Good thing you hadn't washed your clothes. The lab results are unambiguous."

"And what happens now?"

"We'll keep you informed, Ms. Matuschek."

The two detectives took their leave.

"Doesn't surprise me that she can't remember," Nik remarked once they were in the elevator. "Alcohol, shock, darkness . . . was worth a shot, though."

Jasmin drove them toward Schütte's neighborhood, a run-down area in the north part of town. They found parking right in front of Schütte's building, which, like all the others on his street, was covered in graffiti.

There was no Schütte listed on the door panel, so they started on the ground floor and worked their way up. Only one apartment in the entire building didn't have a name on the door, so they tried their luck and rang the doorbell. No answer. They knocked once, then again, harder.

The door across the hallway opened. Nik estimated that the neighbor regarding him from the doorway was in her early twenties. Long, greasy blonde hair; one partially healed black eye. A toddler with a jam-smeared mouth clung to her gray jogging pants; a second child was balanced on her arm.

"The hell's all the noise for?"

Nik pulled out his badge. "We'd like to speak to Mr. Schütte. Does he live here?"

"He ain't here."

"Do you know where he is?"

"Where else? Last Nickel, where he always is."

"Last Nickel?"

"Yeah, the bar around the corner. The Last Nickel."

"Where is it exactly?"

"Left out the building, then left again. It's right there."

Didn't sound difficult. "Thanks very much."

"And tell him when he comes back wasted, he better get the right apartment door, or he'll have my husband to answer to," she called after the two detectives.

"She has quite a pretty face," Nik said.

"Yeah, I noticed. But how can someone let herself go that much?"

The Last Nickel turned out to be just the kind of dark, grimy hole-in-the-wall that Nik had expected.

A large, handwritten "Smoking Allowed" sign on the front door alerted visitors to what to expect inside. Even so, the wall of cigarette smoke, bodily odors, and alcohol fumes practically knocked the detectives back. And it was barely lunchtime.

Glazed eyes fixed on the new arrivals. If the scene was making Nik a little queasy, how uncomfortable was Jasmin feeling? She was the only woman in the whole place.

None of the guys at the bar looked anything like the man they were searching for. One after another, they turned their eyes away as Nik scrutinized their faces. Despite their varying stages of inebriation, they seemed to intuit the nature of his visit.

Nik coughed; Jasmin clapped him gently on the back. They went farther inside. Schütte was sitting at one of the tables. There was no doubt about it. He looked just like the photo.

Two other men were seated at Schütte's table. One was holding a dice cup in one hand and covering the top with the other. He froze in place when he spotted Nik.

"Moritz Schütte?" asked Nik.

"Who wants t'know?"

"Detective Niklas Steg." Niklas presented his badge. "Berlin State Office of Criminal Investigation."

Although Schütte probably had the same blood alcohol level as the others, he appeared sober enough to evaluate the situation. Jasmin moved around behind him as a precaution.

"We have a few questions for you."

Schütte's gaze shifted past Nik to the point in the haze where the exit would normally be visible. It was obvious he was mulling the option of leaping up and making a run for it.

Jasmin positioned herself to be able to push him right back into the chair. Even if she only stopped him temporarily, he'd still have to get past Nik.

Schütte stalled for time. "I ain't got no secrets from my friends," he declared jovially. "Ask yer questions."

"They are in regard to events that occurred in the rose garden in Tiergarten."

Schütte paled. To Nik it seemed as if he'd been expecting a different accusation. Might be worth following up on that later.

"Whatever happened there, I didn' have nothin' to do with it."

"I don't think it's in your interest to discuss this here."

Schütte tried again: "What if I say I ain't comin'?"

"We could place you under provisional arrest."

"You ain't got nothin' on me," snapped Schütte.

"Hmm, let's start with illegal gambling," Jasmin broke in. In a completely pointless maneuver, Schütte's friend hid the dice cup underneath the table.

"Give it a rest, Mr. Schütte. You can come along with us voluntarily or . . ."

Schütte hesitated. Perhaps he was trying to decide which of the two alternatives made him look better in front of his buddies. "'Kay, fine," he conceded at last.

"If you'd be so kind as to accompany us, in that case."

CHAPTER 18

Niklas Steg had invited her out for coffee sooner than Sabrina had been expecting. Café Einstein was on Kurfürstenstraße, not even ten minutes from her place, but Sabrina had been there only two or three times. Nik had chosen it. Over the past few years, one long-established traditional café after another had closed its doors in the western part of Berlin. Café Einstein was one of the last remaining. The place had an expensive, exclusive air to it, old-fashioned and charming. A haunt for the moneyed class, or for people aspiring to it.

Sabrina thanked the waiter who pulled back her chair in a polished manner to seat her. Prices on the menu started well above other restaurants in the area. Having coffee in such an elegant setting felt luxuriously relaxing to Sabrina. The waiter addressed her as "Madame" when she ordered her latte. That was a first.

Nik spotted her quickly when he came in.

Sabrina, why would you suddenly start thinking about gentle kisses brushed against the back of your hand?

Disappointingly, he left it at a handshake. "I'm very glad you could come. Have you been waiting long?"

"Not at all." She pictured Nik in a top hat and tails, a Fred Astaire to her Ginger Rogers.

"What are you thinking about?"

She felt herself turning red. "Why?"

"Your smile."

Deflect, Sabrina, deflect. "Oh, I was just thinking about the dates my daughter has set up for me."

"Your daughter sets you up on dates?"

Crap, that really sounded needy. What are you blabbering about, Sabrina?

"Online." *That didn't make it any better.* "Without my knowledge," she added hastily.

"I have a daughter, too. She's a little older than yours."

"You sound a little sad when you say that."

"Tamara's stopped calling me again."

The waiter brought Sabrina's latte; Nik ordered an espresso.

"She still hasn't come to terms with the separation." Nik told her about Hanna, the wife he was separated from but still married to. She'd cheated on him with one of his colleagues in Munich, which was why he'd left his job there as quickly as possible. The death of one of the commissioners here in Berlin around the same time had freed up a position. The heads of the two departments had organized his quick transfer. Nik was originally from Berlin anyway, and his ailing parents needed his help these days. Without him there, they'd have had to move into a home.

Sabrina felt heartened that Nik was opening up to her about such personal things. At the same time, it reminded her she ought to call her mother. The problem was that her mother annoyed her to no end. Talked her ear off about her gout and other health problems. Their conversations never lasted under an hour. They weren't even conversations, since Sabrina rarely got a word in.

Nik jolted her out of her thoughts. "Tamara is too young to understand how it all works. I've tried to explain it to her."

"She loves her father," Sabrina said. "And she misses him."

"Yeah."

"Well, then, she'll understand someday. Give her time." *Sabrina, you're touched by his worry, have you noticed?* She thought about Herman Munster, her admirer at Heavenly Peace. She liked him, but she realized she wasn't "touched" by him in the same way. Her senses were on heightened alert. *What's going on here? Change the subject, Sabrina.* "How's the woman Mr. Lucke punched?"

"Her nose is broken. It'll take a while for everything to heal, but she's out of the hospital."

"It seemed to me you'd heard the name Annika Weiss before."

"I'm actually not allowed to talk about that."

"Yeah, I know."

He glanced around as though making sure that nobody was listening. "Her husband was murdered a few days ago." In a low voice, he told her about Dominik Weiss's execution. About the words written in blood on the bedroom wall: REAP THE STORM.

Sabrina shuddered, picturing the crime. But she took his breach of police confidentiality as an additional sign of trust.

"And Mrs. Weiss is a suspect? Then why hasn't she been taken in?"

"She has an alibi."

All at once, an idea popped into Sabrina's head: "*Strangers on a Train.*"

"What?"

"*Strangers on a Train.* It's an Alfred Hitchcock movie. A famous tennis player is having problems with his wife and wants to get rid of her. Then when he's on a train, some guy approaches him and says he knows about his misery. The guy promises to kill the wife if the tennis player will kill his father in exchange. That way neither of them has motives for the crimes and they can both make sure they have alibis. Of course, not everything goes according to plan in the end."

"Same as in real life. It looks like Gerd Lucke was the other intended victim, but he's still alive. I'd been thinking much the same thing. Annika Weiss has her husband killed, and in return, she kills Gerd Lucke. But for whom?"

"Who would have a motive for the crime?"

"Could have something to do with Lucke's past."

"That'd be my guess, too."

Sabrina had another idea. "I could check up on Annika Weiss. Call her and ask her how she's doing. And tell her that I think this Lucke guy is repulsive, too, that I just ended up on the case by coincidence." It wouldn't even be a lie.

"I can't ask you to do that."

"You didn't."

"We've had major personnel cuts in the past few years, in every department. Otherwise I'd already have Mrs. Weiss under twenty-four-hour observation."

"Think of it as outsourcing."

"I don't know whether I can officially hire you to do this, let alone pay you."

"We can discuss that later."

"But from what I know of my boss, there's hope at least that he would find the appropriate funding." Nik looked at his watch. "I'm afraid I have to go."

Such a pity, Sabrina mused.

"To the district courthouse. Not a very nice case, either. I'll spare you the details."

"Well, let me just say one thing right off. You don't have to spare me anything."

Oh, that sounded so much more resolute than she'd intended. Hopefully she hadn't scared him off. To her relief, though, he laughed out loud. An elderly woman at the neighboring table scowled at him. Sabrina wanted to be upset at him for laughing at her, but she couldn't do it. Yeah, he definitely touched her more than Herman Munster did.

Nik excused himself, paid for their coffees, and left the café. Sabrina lingered, savoring the ambience of Café Einstein.

CHAPTER 19

FLASHBACK: THE JANA MATUSCHEK CASE

Government authorities had given Jana Matuschek trouble for as long as she could remember. As a child, she'd only skipped school once. She'd heard that her favorite pop idol would be visiting Berlin. Jana, whose bedroom was plastered with posters of the teen celebrity, had wanted more than anything to be at Tegel Airport when his plane landed. Unfortunately, her heartthrob had not appeared—and the airport police had promptly picked the girl up and taken her home. Afterward, she'd been read the riot act three times over: by the police, by school authorities, and by her parents.

She'd known what she'd done wrong even before the first lecture. She'd wished she could cover her ears.

Later—barely of age—she'd applied for a housing subsidy and had to resubmit the form a total of eight times, because the government office had kept finding errors or demanding additional paperwork. It had taken nearly a year before her application was finally approved.

And there were always expenses her friends managed to deduct on their taxes with no problem, but when she tried it, the tax office wouldn't accept them. The nerve-racking appeals procedures that followed usually felt like she was tilting at windmills.

She'd had a similar feeling down at the police station. Not that Detectives Steg and Ibscher had struck her as unlikable or hostile in any way, but the experience had still left her queasy. And there was no way around this trip to the district attorney's office, either.

"Sexual violence against women" was the overarching bureaucratic term for the cases handled by this particular division, the one whose letter requesting her cooperation Jana was now holding. She double-checked the number of the room she stood before, then knocked on the door.

The woman seated at the desk in front of her looked to be in her fifties, with gray hair combed back severely and bright-red lipstick that matched the frames of her cat-eye glasses.

"Yes?"

"Um, I got a letter from a Dr. Margit Castrow-Wille. I have an appointment with her." Jana held the piece of paper out to her.

Ignoring the letter, the attorney held out her hand for Jana to shake. "That's me. Have a seat. Ms. Matuschek, right?"

Jana nodded and sat down.

The district attorney looked at Jana with a friendly smile. "I've already spent a lot of time looking your case over, so you don't have to go over all the details of that horrible night again."

Jana breathed a sigh of relief. She'd experienced numerous flashbacks since the rape, and at least once a week, she woke up drenched in cold sweat, often lying awake until morning. She hoped she never had to talk about the night in the rose garden again.

"But I can't guarantee you won't be questioned about it during the trial."

Jana had been afraid of that, and just imagining the courtroom proceedings sent waves of anxiety through her.

"And you'll have to be in the courtroom at the same time as the defendant," the district attorney added.

"There's no way to avoid that?"

"I'm afraid not. The defendant still denies having committed the crime. And his lawyer will want to question you."

"He denies it?"

"I don't think you have anything to worry about there, Ms. Matuschek. From a legal standpoint, the DNA evidence the police found on your clothing is incontrovertible. The defense doesn't stand a chance. There are dozens of precedent cases."

"So he'll go to prison."

"He's already there. But I don't think he'll be back out for at least two years."

"Two years?" It seemed far too lenient a sentence.

"My experience tells me that's what we'll end up with. I'll ask for a longer sentence, but since the defendant didn't use a gun or any other weapons, I don't think we have much chance of succeeding there."

"What about the belt?" Jana pointed to the bruises still clearly visible around her neck. "He nearly strangled me."

"Attempted murder. That's exactly what I want to argue. I admit I'm not sure it will work. It's even possible that the defendant will get off with just a one-year sentence."

"Just one year?"

"Don't be alarmed, Ms. Matuschek. That shouldn't happen. Given his previous record, the court will probably impose the upper end of the sentence range." The district attorney proceeded to give Jana a basic explanation of the formalities involved in criminal proceedings. "So I can enter you in as a joint plaintiff, right?" she asked when she was finished.

Jana nodded.

"And you should definitely take advantage of your right to criminal compensation. I doubt if the defendant will ever have the resources to pay it, but you never know." The district attorney looked intently into Jana's eyes. "Ms. Matuschek, if you have any additional information that might be of importance to this trial, it's critically important that you share it with me."

Jana hesitated briefly. Then she reached for her handbag. "I've told you everything I know."

CHAPTER 20

Nik would like to have stayed longer at Café Einstein. Being around Sabrina Lampe felt good. The unanswered text messages had long since been forgotten.

On his way to the courthouse, a member of the forensics team called to let him know that the weapon Annika Weiss had threatened Gerd Lucke with was the same one that had been used to shoot her husband. Nik wasn't surprised.

He reached the district court just in time and took a seat next to Jasmin, who greeted him with a silent nod. The district attorney was already in the courtroom, as were Jana Matuschek and her lawyer. Quite a few reporters were present as well; the case had generated a lot of media attention. Jana Matuschek looked exceedingly nervous. Nik had huge respect for her courage in standing up to her rapist.

Now Moritz Schütte was being led into the room as well, accompanied by his lawyer and a uniformed police officer. He was not handcuffed. Jana Matuschek flinched and turned away when she saw him.

Nik looked him over. Schütte looked calm, cool, and collected. He'd seemed down-and-out at the time of his arrest, but now he looked like the perfect son-in-law: parted hair, clean linen trousers, a freshly ironed checkered shirt. He'd shaved, too—something he hadn't done in several days the last time Nik had seen him. Not bad, Nik had to admit. His defense attorney had advised him well.

The attorney himself walked into the room with head held high, not deigning to glance at the prosecution for even a moment. Everything about the way he moved, the way he sat down to whisper with the defendant, suggested arrogance and self-assurance.

Now the door to the judge's chambers opened, and the courtroom went quiet. Everyone stood. The judge—who looked close to retirement age—took his seat and opened the proceedings. After the charges were read out, the district attorney and Ms. Matuschek's lawyer had the floor.

Jana Matuschek elected not to recount the events again herself. Remembering the condition she'd been in, Nik could understand her decision perfectly well. It was hard enough reliving it when others testified about it.

Nik and Jasmin were called to the stand, one after the other, and gave identical accounts of how they'd questioned Jana Matuschek, investigated the crime scene, and subsequently arrested Moritz Schütte.

Silvie Kessler was called next. She told the court about spending the evening at her place, drinking wine with her friend Jana.

The judge listened attentively, asking occasional follow-up questions and nodding in response to the witnesses' replies. He took extensive notes. After the prosecution rested, he invited the defense to start presenting their case.

"My client does not deny the occurrence of the event as such," the defense attorney began.

How would he? Nik thought. Schütte had left plenty of DNA at the scene and on Ms. Matuschek.

"But there is one very grave discrepancy regarding the circumstances under which the event occurred." His expression and body language reflected total self-confidence. A murmur went through the courtroom.

"What do you mean?" the judge asked.

Then he dropped the bomb: "The intercourse was entirely consensual."

Jana Matuschek went pale; her jaw dropped. She began to stand up, but her lawyer put a hand on her shoulder and indicated she should stay seated.

"You heard right," the defense attorney continued. "My client, Mr. Schütte, did not force the joint plaintiff into intercourse. She offered it to him."

It occurred to Nik that the man had named his own client by name, but not Jana Matuschek. To what end? The defense strategy was completely transparent. Nik was sure that Ms. Matuschek's lawyer had described the events in sufficient detail and that his and Jasmin's testimony had been completely believable.

"That contradicts everything we've heard so far," the judge said.

"Precisely," Schütte's attorney replied.

"Objection," Jana's lawyer broke in.

The judge overruled her and signaled for the defense attorney to continue.

"My client, Mr. Schütte, was indeed in Tiergarten's rose garden on the evening in question. You see, Your Honor, he'd been to two job interviews. He'd had a hard day. That evening, he just wanted to go out and get some air. He was enjoying the peace and quiet in Tiergarten so much that he lost track of time. There's nothing illegal about that."

"The incident occurred well after midnight."

"Mr. Schütte fell asleep on a park bench in the rose garden. As I said, he'd had a long day. One of the interviews was in Potsdam, the other in Cottbus. You're welcome to check. He was genuinely tired that evening."

Nik doubted the judge would fall for such a cheap line of argumentation. And as if on cue, a look of skepticism crossed the judge's face.

"Mr. Schütte awoke when he felt someone touching his thigh," the defense attorney went on. "Alarmed, he opened his eyes to discover a heavily made-up woman sitting beside him."

That was news to Nik. At the station, Jana Matuschek had seemed attractive but withdrawn, the way she was today in court. Of course, there was no way to prove what she'd looked like the night of the crime. It was her word against his.

"She also smelled heavily of alcohol," he added, turning to Silvie Kessler. "As we've already heard from her friend, she and the plaintiff consumed a great deal of red wine that night. And who knows if they even remember what else they drank while they were at it."

An uneasy feeling arose in Nik. The defense attorney was actually succeeding in twisting things around and stirring up doubt. And he didn't like it.

Schütte's lawyer turned to address the judge directly again. "I apologize for putting this so bluntly, but the plaintiff made Mr. Schütte an offer he could hardly misunderstand. Fifty with condom, a hundred without."

"Objection!" cried Jana Matuschek's lawyer.

The judge leaned back and looked at Jana. "Is this the truth, Ms. Matuschek?"

Jana Matuschek struggled for words, her cheeks reddened, she wiped her eyes.

"Ms. Matuschek? Would you answer the question please?"

"No, it's not the truth," she whispered.

"Could you please speak up?"

"No," she spoke up, "it is not the truth."

"May I ask the plaintiff a question?" Schütte's attorney broke in, and the judge nodded.

"Since you don't deny having been very drunk that night, can you remember everything that happened in the rose garden?"

Jana Matuschek hesitated. She turned to the judge for help, but he was silent.

"Well?" asked the defense attorney. "I'm listening?"

"I can't remember everything."

"Could you please speak up?" The defense counsel repeated the judge's exact words.

"I can't remember everything."

He paused for a moment to let her words sink in. "After making the offer, the plaintiff unzipped Mr. Schütte's pants and took hold of his penis. He had no idea what was happening."

"Objection!" called the state prosecutor.

"Sustained," agreed the judge. "We will continue this in a closed session."

But Schütte's attorney didn't let up: "I have evidence proving that this woman works as a prostitute. She also needs money for drugs."

What a turn of events. Nik didn't believe a word of the crap the defense attorney was spewing. But then he looked at Jana Matuschek and registered the look on her face—as if she felt she'd been caught red-handed—and suddenly he wasn't so sure anymore.

CHAPTER 21

FLASHBACK: THE JANA MATUSCHEK CASE

The man in the red Opel Astra cruised slowly down the road, eyeing the women standing on the sidewalk. Most of them looked him square in the face, smiled seductively, and mouthed things the driver couldn't hear but still understood. There was a girl to suit every john's preference. It didn't matter if a guy liked them slim or Rubenesque, blonde, brunette, or redhead. In leather and vinyl or the housewife type. This street had them all.

The driver liked the girl in front of a furniture store on the corner. Small, thin, heavily made-up. A tight pink top that only just concealed her breasts. White leather shorts riding up her buttocks. Knee-length boots in the same color. At first he put her at twenty-one, but when he looked more closely, he knew she was younger.

But even if he'd known she wasn't sixteen yet, he wouldn't have cared. On the contrary, the younger, the better.

He pulled over and braked, put the passenger-side window down. The girl approached and leaned her head in. "What do you say, handsome, you interested?" The answer was written all over his face, and she kept talking: "Thirty marks for a blow job. Fucking is eighty." Without waiting for an answer, she opened the car door and got in. She gave him directions to an old villa on a dead-end street. They didn't talk during the short drive; it seemed to her that the john already knew the way to the place.

They walked to the entrance, the girl thankful that someone was keeping an eye on her from behind the curtains on the ground floor. This man made sure that no one gave the girls any trouble, a service for which they paid him a cut of their earnings. Much too large a cut, in her view, but she had little choice. Prostitution had been her sole source of income since her father had thrown her out. Told her to get her own place because she'd been in his new girlfriend's way. Just eighteen months before, all had been right with her world—her mother still alive, the devastating cancer suspected by no one.

The system at the villa was a simple one: if the door was open, the room was available. The first three doors were shut, but they had better luck at the fourth. The girl sat on the bed and addressed her customer. "Well," she asked, "what are you into?"

"Do you take drugs?" he asked.

"What?"

"The Band-Aid in the crook of your arm."

"Oh, that. No, no, I gave blood today," she lied, suspecting the man could see right through it. But he didn't push the issue. It didn't seem to bother him.

"My fantasies are a little unusual," he said.

Not something she had much experience with yet. But she knew that everything outside the norm paid more. And she wanted to get her own place as soon as possible. The friend she was staying with was getting on her nerves. Her apartment was unbelievably cramped, and the friend was always sermonizing, wouldn't believe her repeated vow to quit turning tricks as soon as she'd saved up the money she needed for a normal life. But that truly was her plan—first earn enough money, then quit prostitution for good. For her mother. And to show her father she could get along fine without him.

Time to grin and bear it, she told herself.

"It's nothing too bad," the john said.

That's relative, she thought. "What is it you have in mind?"

He approached her; involuntarily, she scooted back a little. He reached out and caressed her throat with one hand, while undoing his zipper with the other. Then he pushed her down, and she simply lay there, motionless. As he penetrated her, he wrapped both hands around her throat—and squeezed. She could feel immediately how much that turned him on.

She wanted to scream, but she couldn't breathe. Everything started to go black. He let her grab a quick breath before tightening his grip again. She heard him moan in pleasure; then she passed out.

Slaps to the face woke her. Her throat hurt. When she opened her eyes, he stopped slapping her and began waving a two-hundred-mark bill in front of her face. "You've already earned this. If we can go a little further, you'll get two hundred more."

Fifteen-year-old Jana Matuschek thought about her own apartment, about her future.

She nodded.

CHAPTER 22

Jana Matuschek left the courtroom in a daze. She heard the district attorney speaking to her with a reproachful look on her face, but the words did not register. She neither shook the woman's hand nor said good-bye, merely turned and left the lawyer standing in the stairwell of the courthouse. She just wanted to get out, out into the fresh air. Her past had caught up to her. Once in the gutter, always in the gutter? Had it really been necessary for her to talk about her old life? No, it was nobody's business! It had nothing to do with the rape, not one thing!

"Ms. Matuschek?"

She picked up her pace. The street to her right led toward the Victory Column, which was near the rose garden. No way she was going there. *Straight ahead. Just go straight ahead.* She saw green leafy trees in that direction. She took a deep breath, fought back her tears. She wasn't going to show weakness to anyone. Never again.

"Ms. Matuschek?"

The street was uphill, but she walked faster anyway.

Was somebody talking? Yet another person who wanted something from her? No more explaining, no more defending herself.

"Wait, Ms. Matuschek! I'm a friend!"

Faster, away from the voice.

But the stranger caught up to her, planted herself directly in front of Jana. Jana ignored her, stepped to one side. The woman blocked her path. Jana looked into her eyes. She seemed serious and decisive. *Just let me pass,* Jana thought.

"I followed the trial, Ms. Matuschek."

A reporter? Jana was silent.

"I can help you."

Nobody can do that.

"That pig won't get away with this."

Later, soaking in the tub, that was the only sentence Jana remembered. The rest of the encounter with the unfamiliar woman she let vanish from memory. The letter she'd left behind on a stool was already gone from memory as well.

"That pig won't get away with this."

In what had been her life, Jana Matuschek recalled reading that the subconscious refused to accept negation, refused to process words like *no* and *none*, wouldn't consent to them. Not thinking about a pink elephant was impossible. And so the woman's words morphed in her mind.

"That pig will get away with this."

Yeah, the pig had already gotten away with it. When the verdict was announced, Schütte had looked straight at her and smiled.

That was when she'd finally recognized him, from back then, from her time as a prostitute. And in that moment, she'd known it was all over. Her past had officially caught up to her.

She ran her fingertips over the razor blade in her hand, slicing open the tip of her index finger.

Jana's innocence hadn't been taken from her in the rose garden. She'd lost it years ago, working the street. Since then, every man had been able to take whatever he wanted from her.

She felt worthless. The will to keep fighting—against her father, her stepmother, the defense attorney, the judge, Moritz Schütte, the violent demons of her past—that will was gone, imploded. She was tired of fighting.

She slit her wrists with the razor blade. Lengthwise—that went faster. She watched as swirls of blood created patterns in the warm bathwater. Then she drifted off.

CHAPTER 23

Plenty of women would have been afraid to walk around in Hasenheide Park at night. Not Jennifer. Jennifer had a goal. And fear didn't enter into it. The last time she'd been afraid was as a little girl. Afraid of her father. But that was a long time ago, more than twenty years.

She'd cultivated qualities that blocked out the fear. A sense of justice. Empathy for those who'd suffered the same fate. An unshakeable desire for retribution and the need to punish the transgressor. The fear disappeared behind them all; Jennifer didn't give it an inch of space. She strode confidently down the path into the park, back straight, head held high. Her destination was not a location, but a person.

Several people approached her to ask if she needed anything. Hashish, mostly; one guy offered LSD, another crystal meth. Most of the dealers were African or Eastern European. The drug scene was a problem the police had no idea how to solve. They conducted raids every so often, arrested the dealers or sent them back to their home countries. But nothing seemed to change about the scene in Hasenheide Park. One dealer disappeared, another took his place. How the drugs and the dealers reached Berlin remained a mystery.

Drugs, however, weren't what Jennifer was in the market for. The man she was seeking was black and had a two-inch scar on his right cheek. She hoped he wasn't among those who'd landed in jail or been deported. She would recognize him as soon as she saw him.

And there he was, standing under a majestic old chestnut tree, not far from the place where she'd met him the first time. As soon as he saw her, he moved as though to disappear into the bushes. But she slowed down as she approached, to signal that she wasn't a threat. On the contrary.

He waited.

"I need a gun," Jennifer said without preamble.

The man looked her over, squinting. "You here already, few days before," he said in an accent that Jennifer couldn't place. She didn't reply. "I sell you Makarov, with silencer," he remembered.

"I need another one."

"What about other?"

"Do you have another one for me or not?"

"Russian friend have lots."

"Then get me one," Jennifer said. She rummaged in her handbag and pulled out several hundred-euro bills. "You'll get the rest tomorrow when I pick up the gun."

"Second gun cost more," he countered, trying his luck. "I not know where first gun come from."

"How much?"

"Five hundred."

Jennifer hesitated but didn't feel it was worth haggling.

"Meet here tomorrow," the man said, "same time."

She nodded and went her way. An onlooker would assume she was merely out for a walk, never imagining she'd just purchased a handgun, one she intended to put to use soon. Her mother's last words echoed in her mind: "Sometimes it's important to do things that have to be done."

CHAPTER 24

FLASHBACK: THE
JENNIFER CASE

When the girl came home, she found her mother dead, hanging from the ceiling.

She'd hurried up the stairs of the apartment building, taking two at a time, proud and excited. She'd gotten an A and a B that morning at school and was looking forward to telling her mother. When she reached the apartment door, she pulled the key out of her pocket and tilted it back and forth in her hand. She was about to unlock the door by herself for the first time. Her parents had finally decided to trust her with her own key the day before. She'd gone right over to practice a few times in her mother's presence, and now she managed to unlock it on the first try. Beaming, she walked into the apartment.

The girl set her heavy backpack beside the coat rack and called out for her mother. "Mom! I'm home!"

No answer. And no mother coming out to return the girl's cheerful greeting.

"Mom?" The girl's voice grew quieter, her steps more hesitant, as she walked down the long hallway of the old apartment. To her right, the door to her parents' bedroom was open, but it was empty.

"Mom?" The girl knocked cautiously on the bathroom door. "Are you in there?"

The stillness frightened the girl. Slowly she approached the kitchen and stepped through the doorway. She saw her mother's white socks at eye level.

The girl's eyes drifted upward. Her mother was wearing the lilac summer dress that the girl liked so much. Her long blonde hair was swirling around her shoulders as it always did. But her mother's eyes were no longer the ones she knew. They were bulging out of their sockets, and they were staring straight ahead, dull and expressionless, fixed on a point above the girl's head. Her mother's jaw was hanging open, the tip of her tongue peeping out. Her face looked puffy and had a faintly violet shimmer to it. An unpleasant smell made the girl wrinkle her nose.

"Mom?"

The girl thought she had asked the question aloud again, but she hadn't heard any sound come out of her mouth. She looked down at the ground. A kitchen chair had fallen over underneath her mother. Next to it was a pair of red lacquer shoes, one tipped onto its side. The girl looked at her own feet. She was wearing the same shoes, only smaller.

When she raised her eyes again, she remembered the way her mother had looked and sounded that morning. "You have to be strong, honey." Then she had bent down and stroked her daughter's cheek tenderly. "You have to learn to tell the difference. Between good and evil." She'd said those words to her daughter very quietly, as though the apartment walls might be listening in on them. "Sometimes it's important to do things that have to be done."

The words still echoed in her head. And then one last affectionate kiss on the lips before the girl had left for school. A good-bye kiss like the ones she'd gotten on every other school day. Only now did the girl realize that it had felt different, tasted different. Saltier, somehow.

The girl paused uncertainly. Then she blocked everything out. "I got an A in English," she said, "and a B in math." She avoided looking her mother in the face.

Her stomach growled. She remembered that her mother had wanted to heat up the leftover casserole from the night before. She walked over to the refrigerator—giving the chair, the lacquer shoes, and her mother a wide berth—and pulled out the black enamel pot. The girl was forbidden to use the gas stove, and it was a rule she obeyed. So she set the cold casserole on the kitchen table.

"I'll set the table for us, okay?"

She took three plates out of the cupboard—one for herself, one for her father, and one for her mother—and fetched a ladle and three soupspoons from the silverware drawer. Then she took three napkins out of another drawer and folded them the way the crafts teacher had shown them in class. She set everything out on the table neatly, as she'd been taught. Then she realized that only two people would be able to sit down, so she righted the chair that had fallen over. Now everything was perfect.

The girl took her seat. Her stomach grumbled again, but she didn't eat. For several minutes, she stared at the enamel pot. Then, slowly, she turned her head back toward her mother. Now the dead woman's back was to her, but it felt like her eyes were staring straight through her lifeless body. The girl stayed where she was—until she heard a noise.

A key. It turned in the lock, and the apartment door clicked open. Dad. Now that he was home, they'd finally be able to eat. She heard the familiar sound of his slow, heavy footsteps, and then her father appeared in the doorway. The girl now had both parents in view.

Her father's briefcase fell to the ground. His pupils dilated. No scream came out of his open mouth.

"I already put food out on the table, Dad."

Her father studied her mother's lifeless body; then his gaze wandered down to her feet, and finally over to his daughter. The girl gave him a smile.

"There's casserole," she said, gesturing to the enamel pot.

The color drained out of her father's face, then returned after a few seconds. He regarded his wife's face with curiosity, narrowing his eyes. His bushy brows rose a shade. With one finger, he carefully prodded his wife's left foot up against her right. The body began to sway slightly.

"Cold, unfortunately," the girl remarked, referring to their meal.

His left hand stroked her white sock tenderly, then her calf; his right hand was twitching. The girl watched the way he pressed his lips together as he continued to stare at the dead woman's face. His grip tightened around his wife's ankle. At the same time, his right hand drifted toward his crotch. The girl saw that a bulge was beginning to form in her father's pants. She was frightened, because she knew what that meant.

"Mmm," went her father, blinking. Now his fingers were drumming gently against the bulge.

You have to be strong, honey, the girl heard her mother's voice say.

She slid off the chair and backed away from her father.

His eyes drifted from his wife's face to that of his daughter.

You have to learn to tell the difference. Between good and evil.

The girl's retreat ended two steps later, when she felt the kitchen cupboard door against her back.

Her father let go of her mother's foot and walked slowly past the corpse. His eyes remained fixed on the girl. He fumbled at his zipper.

Sometimes it's important to do things that have to be done.

"Please don't," said the girl.

"Mmm."

Then the girl closed her eyes.

CHAPTER 25

Just to be on the safe side, Nik put on gloves. It was easy to get hurt doing this kind of work. He reached for the garden shears, which were stiff and squeaky. After oiling them, he turned his attention to the roses in his parents' garden.

"This is the first time I've ever done this," he said, gripping one of the thorny stalks.

"I know," he heard his father say behind him. "But it was definitely . . ." Karl Steg grasped for the right word. "Overdue." His father still spoke slowly, pausing frequently, as though gathering up the words he needed one by one. Even so, the difference was like night and day compared to his condition a few weeks before. The doctors had predicted his dad would probably recover from his stroke as long as he didn't give up trying, but Nik hadn't wanted to get his hopes up too much, just in case. He was walking better now, too. Nik had built wooden ramps at the front and terrace doors, so that Karl could get in and out with his walker. Steps remained an insurmountable obstacle.

"Is this right?" asked Nik, snipping off one of the old shoots.

"Yeah."

The ramp leading from the terrace to the garden had disappeared three times; once Nik had found it in a Dumpster three days later. Finally, he'd decided to screw it on.

His mother was already walking up and down it as though it had always been there. But at first, she'd insisted on disposing of the "foreign object." Explaining things to her seldom brought results anymore. As long as his father's condition didn't worsen, though, Nik was optimistic that his parents could manage on their own when he was on duty.

"I just couldn't stand to see the rose bushes like that anymore."

Nik took it as a positive sign that his dad was once again showing an interest in his beloved garden, and he was happy to help. As recently as last summer, his father had taken care of it on his own. The garden now wasn't what Nik would call overgrown, but it had certainly seen better days under Karl Steg's care.

"Nicky!" Nik heard his mother call in a reproachful tone. He turned around to see her marching down the ramp. She had a jar in one hand. "I told you not to go outside and play without protection." She removed the lid and scooped out a glob. Nik shut his eyes and submitted to his mother rubbing the lotion on his face. She didn't forget his neck, either.

"Much better."

He peered at the label on the jar. Hand cream. *Could have been worse,* he thought. Although her husband was sitting directly in front of her, facing the sun, she walked right past him back into the house. Karl just shrugged his shoulders, and Nik went back to the flowers.

"Tell me about . . . the trial . . . Jana . . ."

"Matuschek," Nik finished for him.

Karl Steg had been on the force as well, though never as highly ranked as his son was now—a fact the father was extremely proud of. Nik, ignoring official protocol, told him about his work every day and sensed that his stories helped boost his father's will to live.

Now, as he trimmed the roses, he recounted the trial in meticulous detail, describing everyone involved and explaining the surprising turn the proceedings had taken. Told him how Jasmin's hands had balled into fists when the verdict had been read out, how her eyes shot daggers at the vile Schütte. Jana Matuschek, on the other hand, had merely sat there, miserable, eyes lowered in shame.

Schütte himself had no doubt been instructed not to make his joy too obvious. He'd remained coolly composed throughout his trial, as if butter wouldn't melt in his mouth.

Nik's fears had been confirmed. It had been her word against his. Jana Matuschek's past, regrettably, had been nearly as questionable as Moritz Schütte's. If the judge had seen Jana when she'd initially told the detectives about the rape, there wouldn't have been a doubt in his mind that she was telling the truth, regardless of how much she'd had to drink. Innocent until proven guilty, however. The judge had had no choice.

"Deserving justice and getting justice—" Karl Steg began.

"Aren't always the same thing, I know," Nik finished the thought for him. "But it hurts to see it in real life."

His father grunted in agreement.

As far as his gardening work was concerned, on the other hand, Nik was quite satisfied with the results. He took a step back and regarded the roses. "So? Not bad, huh?"

"Mmm, well . . . ," his father said, "it will do for now."

His mother's voice rang out from the house. "Come inside, Nicky. Time to eat. There's mashed potatoes."

Nik hated mashed potatoes. He'd hated them as a kid, too. Same with the liverwurst sandwiches his mother had always packed for his lunch. Now that he was living at home again, his mother had resumed supplying them on a daily basis. Resistance was futile.

Nik helped his father stand, and they went inside. Into the house the couple had bought when they were young, the house Nik had grown up in.

CHAPTER 26

The woman had spent enough time observing the dilapidated building in the working-class neighborhood of Wedding. She didn't see any "Schütte" on the doorbell panel; all the names listed sounded foreign. But she had already learned that he lived on the second floor. The fact that the door to the building didn't lock correctly anymore wasn't news to her, either. Nobody was interested in repairing it. Who would want to steal anything from this building? And more to the point, what was there to steal?

Schütte had left the building ten minutes before. He'd gone into his usual bar, the Last Nickel. The woman had watched him. She knew he wouldn't be back for a while, just like all the other nights. So she took her time, walked calmly up the stairs to the second floor. She paused, listening for any noise—the building was silent. She took out her lock pick and inserted it in the keyhole. The building had to be fifty years old at least, and in that time, she doubted that a single apartment owner or tenant had bothered to install a modern, burglarproof lock. The woman gave the lock pick a quarter turn, and the door clicked open. Child's play.

The place reeked of stale air, cigarette smoke, booze, and man sweat. The woman shuddered. She wished she could open all the windows, but someone outside might see her. And Schütte might notice the unusually fresh air when he walked in. No, it was crucial that he didn't suspect anything.

She sat down on the edge of a disgusting armchair and laid out her mask and handgun, then attached the silencer. Then she waited, patiently, for more than three hours.

When she heard Schütte opening the door, she put the mask on and picked up the weapon. Schütte appeared in the doorway, stinking of beer and Jägermeister. He blinked. Was he so drunk he thought his mind was playing tricks on him?

"Whadya want?" He was swaying a little but had hardly slurred his words.

She gave him a moment to focus.

He looked the unfamiliar woman up and down. "We at a Mardi Gras party or somethin'?"

He started to take a step forward, and the woman snapped, "Stay where you are!" She clicked off the safety and aimed straight at Schütte's chest. "I mean it."

He froze in place. "Who're you?"

"Don't you recognize it?"

"That a Greek mask?"

"I'm surprised you can tell."

Schütte shrugged. "That supposed to scare me or somethin'?"

"It's a Greek goddess. Can you guess which one?"

"Oh, now we're playing *Who Wants to Be a Millionaire*. Can I call a friend?" Was he actually grinning? This wasn't going the way the woman had imagined. She wanted to see Schütte shaking in his boots. And suffering. But he wasn't doing her the favor. Not yet.

She tilted her gun and aimed a couple of feet lower. "Getting shot in the balls doesn't kill you right away. First, you bleed severely. And if the bleeding can't be stopped, you spend some time dying an extremely painful death." That wiped the smug look off his face. "This isn't a game."

He stood, silent.

She gestured to her mask with her free hand. "Nemesis, the Greek goddess of revenge."

His knitted brow told her that he was racking his brain.

"You Matuschek?"

"No," said the woman, quickly and sharply. "You're defiling her name just by saying it."

"So you know her?"

She realized she'd given herself away, but she didn't care.

"Or it really is you?"

"I am Nemesis, the goddess of retribution."

"Retribution? What for?"

"For your crime. Nemesis is not as merciful as the judges in the District Court of Tiergarten."

"Matuschek's a whore. Judge saw it, too. She came up to me in the rose garden and—"

"Shut up!"

He flinched.

"That's a lie. And you know it."

Schütte was trembling.

"Maybe I'll make it quick and painless. But you need to repent."

"Repent? For what? Fuckin' a hooker?"

She was a heartbeat away from pulling the trigger. Why was he still so brazen? In court, too, he'd been arrogantly relaxed. And he'd been sober then. Now, wasted, he seemed to have himself equally under control. He knew exactly what he was doing. And he'd known what he was doing in the rose garden. The woman didn't doubt it for a second. "All right then. You've chosen the painful version."

"Gimme a break. You had yer fun, whoever you are. Just get out an' we'll forget this whole thing. I won't even remember you tomorrow."

"No, you won't remember me tomorrow. There will be nothing left for you to remember with. But before the shot to your brain, we'll start with another part of your anatomy. How sad you didn't keep your urges under better control."

And with that, she pulled the trigger. And finally, finally, she saw fear in his eyes, if only for the fraction of a second before it gave way to pain. He screamed.

The silencer ensured that no one would have heard the shot, but the shrieking would alert all his neighbors. She had to end this, fast. Which was too bad, because she wanted to watch him writhe in agony on the floor awhile longer. She put the gun to his head and pulled the trigger.

Blood was pooling on the floor. There was no time to lose. She dipped two fingers into it and left her calling card on the wall: REAP THE STORM.

CHAPTER 27

Sabrina Lampe's stomach was grumbling. She shifted from one foot to the other. The apartment complex Annika Weiss lived in was within view. She'd actually planned on just keeping an eye on it for a while. Trusting her luck. Waiting for Inspector Luck and Sergeant Chance to hurry to her rescue. For Annika Weiss to leave home so she could follow her and observe her. Maybe she'd meet up with someone suspicious looking—with the "stranger on the train," as Sabrina had mentally dubbed the other person, her own loose interpretation of the fateful encounter in the Alfred Hitchcock film.

She hadn't come up with any better strategies. And at the moment, she wasn't thinking all that clearly anyway. When she wasn't preoccupied with thoughts of Inspector Luck and Sergeant Chance's colleague Detective Niklas Steg, she worried about the way her stomach was acting up.

Suddenly, in a flash of insight, she realized what was causing it. "The folic acid," she said aloud. A woman walking past looked momentarily startled. She probably thought Sabrina was one of the city's many mentally ill, whom it was wise not to provoke.

It was Mojito who had told her about folic acid. "The folic acid has practically no side effects, Ms. Lampe. Maybe one person in a thousand gets diarrhea."

Bingo.

Mojito was her fifteen-year-old daughter's boyfriend. Lara idolized him, this scrawny youth who always looked like he needed a good meal.

Puberty, thought Sabrina, *is the phase of life when one's parents become difficult.* Whereas she and Lara were constantly butting heads as a result of said phase, Mojito was always friendly and courteous. Sabrina had never seen him in a bad mood.

"We're going to try the vegetarian thing again, Ms. Lampe," he'd told her a few days before, and Lara had nodded eagerly.

"You two are still growing. You need meat."

Lara pouted.

"No, no, Ms. Lampe, the only important things are protein and folic acid." The first time that unholy name had been spoken in her presence. "But you can get both of those from other sources. Legumes, for example. Tofu and other soy products. Getting enough protein isn't difficult. And there are supplements for the folic acid." He pulled a bottle of pills from his pocket and set them in front of Sabrina on the kitchen table. The label was in a script Sabrina didn't recognize.

"South Korea," Mojito said. "I got them online. Cheaper than drugstores."

Sabrina looked at her daughter.

"This time I'm not going to let you tempt me," Lara told her. "Steak, roast beef, schnitzel, I don't care. I'm not eating meat anymore."

"Lara—" Sabrina was about to start lecturing her, but Mojito interrupted.

"Why don't you join us, Ms. Lampe?" He gave her a charming smile.

Sabrina could understand why her daughter was in love with him. And in principle, he was right about Germans eating far too much meat. But giving it up completely? She couldn't imagine herself doing that.

"Yeah, Mom, do it with us. I bet you can't last four weeks."

"Oh, you think, huh?" *Crap. Shouldn't have said that.*

"Okay, let's make a deal," Lara said. "You don't eat meat for four weeks. If you make it, then I'll eat meat once a week."

Sabrina saw that Lara was actually creating a loophole for herself. Her daughter liked meat far too much to stick to a completely vegetarian diet for long. This way she could save face in front of Mojito.

Mojito smiled. Like always.

"All right," Sabrina replied. "I'm in."

"The folic acid has practically no side effects, Ms. Lampe," Mojito told her as he opened the bottle and pushed one of the pills across the table. "Maybe one person in a thousand gets diarrhea."

And here she was, fourteen days later, standing in front of Annika Weiss's apartment building in Pankow, with only one thought in her head: *Where can I find a toilet?*

There were no public facilities anywhere in sight. And no bushes for her to disappear behind unnoticed. Onward and upward, that was her only alternative.

She hurried to the building door and rang Annika Weiss's doorbell repeatedly. When the door finally opened, Sabrina rushed up the stairs, clenching what were currently her most important muscles.

"I'm the woman who found you at Gerd Lucke's place and called the ambulance," she said in explanation as she practically threw Mrs. Weiss aside and started opening doors until she found the bathroom. Just in time.

Now she relaxed and closed her eyes. She fantasized about Kim Jong-un's missiles blowing up the entire South Korean pharmaceutical industry.

"Just you wait, Lara," she muttered to herself. "Mom's cooking your favorite dish tonight. We'll see how strong your resolve is once those delicious smells fill the apartment."

"Everything okay?" she heard Annika Weiss call from the other side of the door.

"Just you wait, Mojito."

"You mean you had too many cocktails last night?"

Had she just said that out loud? "Um, everything's fine. Just a moment, please." She finished up, washed her hands, and left the bathroom.

Annika Weiss was waiting in the hallway. A large bandage covered her nose. She regarded the unexpected visitor with wide eyes.

"Sorry for barging in like that," Sabrina said. "I was just in the area, and I really needed to . . ."

"Yes, I see. But apart from that, was there something you wanted?"

"I just wanted to tell you that I don't have anything to do with that Lucke guy."

"And you came all the way here just to tell me that? How do you even know where I live?"

"Oh, I wanted to visit you in the hospital, but you'd already been let out. And I just happened to see your address." Sometimes she surprised herself how readily she could lie.

Annika Weiss nodded.

"Lucke's a friend of my ex-husband's."

"Doesn't speak in your ex-husband's favor."

Sabrina laughed. "Trust me, there are plenty of things that don't speak in my ex-husband's favor."

"My husband was murdered a few days ago."

"Yes, I know. My condolences."

Mrs. Weiss let it go at that. "What do you want from me?"

"I don't suppose you've got any tea? My stomach . . ."

Annika Weiss knitted her brow.

"Trust me, I'm on your side. Lucke's a pig. I know what he did."

"All right," Mrs. Weiss relented. "Come into the living room. I'll make us some chamomile tea. That's supposed to be good for your stomach. I have some melba toast, too."

Sabrina breathed a sigh of relief. Not only was she getting the opportunity to talk to Annika Weiss, but there was a toilet nearby. She heard her hostess milling about in the kitchen and took a good look around the living room. A thick book sitting atop a chest of drawers caught her eye. It didn't look like it normally belonged there. It was a Bible. Sabrina opened it to the page that was bookmarked. A verse had been lightly circled in pencil: "For they have sown the wind, and they shall reap the whirlwind: it hath no stalk; the bud shall yield no meal: if so be it yield, the strangers shall swallow it up." Had Annika Weiss been researching the message written in blood by her husband's killer? Or was there more to it than that?

The sounds from the kitchen stopped. Sabrina shut the Bible and sat on the sofa. Over tea, she did her best to find out what she could from Annika Weiss without arousing suspicion. They talked about her murdered husband. Although Annika praised him to the skies, Sabrina wondered if it wasn't out of self-justification, as though she were searching for reasons why she'd stayed with the man so many years.

At no point in the conversation did the widow seem like she was grieving. On the contrary, Sabrina sensed that the woman was relieved to be rid of her husband and that her marriage had not been a happy one. She would advise Nik to ask the Weisses' friends about that.

Dominik Weiss, it seemed, had not been a particularly good person. Gerd Lucke, either, before he'd gone to prison, anyway. Had the time he served reformed him? Sabrina didn't want to pass judgment yet in that regard. But the parallels in the two stories were hard to ignore. She was becoming more and more convinced of her *Strangers on a Train* theory. All they were missing was the main character, the stranger. That, and a concrete motive.

Did it have something to do with the past? With Lucke's criminal history? If so, Nik would have to sift through those old files. Or was Gerd Lucke guilty of a new offense? Sabrina realized she wouldn't be getting much more in the way of answers. Annika Weiss had herself under control; she knew exactly what she wanted to reveal and what she didn't.

At least Sabrina's stomach was starting to quiet down. She thanked Mrs. Weiss for the tea and took her leave. On her way home, she went over their conversation again in her mind, and a sense of déjà vu crept over her. The visit reminded her of something she'd experienced recently. But what? It wouldn't come to her.

CHAPTER 28

The way Zimmermann squeezed his corpulent figure in behind his desk always reminded Niklas Steg of Jabba the Hutt somehow. All he needed was a scantily clad Princess Leia chained up at his feet. His face, on the other hand, was more like that of the stuffed gorilla sitting on his bookshelf, the one with the word *Boss* on its chest and a cigar in its mouth. Zimmermann's excessive smoking had left its foul taint on his carpet and furniture long ago. He kept his office window open throughout the summer, despite the noise of the traffic, but even that did no good anymore.

Nik and Jasmin had just returned from the crime scene. "Report!" Zimmermann ordered the minute they took their seats in front of his desk.

"The same MO as the Weiss murder," Nik began. "The words *reap the storm* in capital letters over the bed on the wall. Written in the victim's blood. It was a proper execution, no mercy whatsoever." The crime scenes in this series of murders were among the grisliest he had seen in twenty years of service. The images continued to haunt him.

"Once again, the perpetrator didn't bother wearing gloves," added Jasmin, chewing gum.

"Who's the victim?" Zimmermann asked.

"Moritz Schütte. He was the defendant in the rape case Ms. Ibscher and I were called to testify in last week."

"Which gives us a suspect."

"We went by her place on the way back. Nobody answered the door. None of the neighbors know where she is. Hasn't been seen in a few days apparently."

"Might be a sign that it was her."

"We posted Thaler in front of the building. We'll know when she returns. Then we can question her and request a DNA sample. But I have a hard time imagining that she's the murderer."

"Why?"

"It just doesn't seem like something she'd do. I can certainly imagine her losing her head over how the trial turned out, but I can't see her doing anything premeditated."

"You're assuming this was a planned murder, Nik?"

"Yes, we found an identical postcard." Nik held up a plastic baggie. The words *sow the wind* were clearly visible. "It's the third card like this. We found the first one in Dominik Weiss's desk. Gerd Lucke got the second one but threw it out, and this one was lying in a pile of newspapers on Moritz Schütte's living room table. Like I said, announcing plans to kill someone doesn't seem like Jana Matuschek to me."

Nik thought back to Sabrina Lampe's phone call a few hours earlier. She'd located the scripture and wanted to tell him. He'd already found out, but he smiled when he recalled the sound of Sabrina's voice as she recited the verse to him over the phone.

"Could the motive be religious in nature? Is Mrs. Weiss deeply Christian?"

"It can't have been Mrs. Weiss," Jasmin piped up. "Dombrowski's got ears on her phone. At the time of the crime, she was in the middle of a nearly two-hour phone conversation with one of her friends."

"*The Third Man?*" Nik suggested.

"Come again?"

"Another old movie. Like *Strangers on a Train*." He'd already mentioned to his boss in a previous conversation the theory of reciprocal murders and alibis.

"Of course, I know both movies." Zimmermann nodded. "And if it wasn't Mrs. Weiss or Ms. Matuschek, then it must have been a third man—well, third woman—whose identity we have yet to learn. But who?"

"That's the question, boss."

CHAPTER 29

"Sow the wind . . . ," Florian Lorenz read on the postcard he'd found in his mailbox, along with assorted grocery store flyers and a doctor's bill. For just a moment, he wondered if some sect or political group had sent the curious message; then he simply stuck the postcard in among the flyers again. The bill worried him more—his income wasn't keeping up with his expenses as it was.

And his back hurt. Every step he took up the four flights to his apartment caused him pain. Twelve hours of physical labor at the trade-fair center had taken their toll. And it would be the same thing again tomorrow, when everything had to be ready. Nobody wanted the Consumer Electronics Fair to start more than he did. For everyone else, it would be a chance to check out the latest technology; for him it meant that the exhausting setup work was finally over. Afterward he had almost a week off—time to relax, time for his daughters. Then the drudgery would start again with the teardown. But at least the pay was good, and it came on time. So far he'd never had to borrow from anyone. He'd manage to pay the doctor's bill somehow, too.

As soon as he unlocked the door, he heard Melanie's and Sophie's footsteps. The twins ran toward him, beaming, and flung their arms around him. The apartment smelled like pancakes. He bent down and kissed each of the girls on the lips, tasting strawberry jam. Pain shot through his back again as he straightened up, and he let out a groan.

"What's wrong, Daddy?" asked Melanie.

He didn't respond.

Sophie took his hand and tugged on it. "Come on. Grandma's making pancakes. You get the next one."

"Not so fast, I'm coming."

Florian's mother was standing in the kitchen in an apron, a frying pan in one hand. She nodded at him in greeting and lifted a freshly made pancake onto a waiting plate.

"What about my girls?"

"It's your turn, Daddy. I already ate two."

"Me, too."

"What about you, Mom?"

"You go ahead and eat first. Bon appétit." She turned back to the stove and began pouring more batter into the pan.

"Sorry I'm so late today," he told her as he spread jam on his pancake.

"Oh, I know how things are before a big trade fair," she replied. "You've been working there long enough now."

Florian rolled the pancake up, then used his knife and fork to cut off a bite.

"I just pick them up and eat them," Sophie said.

"Me, too. Want me to show you?" Melanie reached out for the pancake, but Florian managed to fend her off. She looked disappointed.

"I know how to do that, Mellie. I just prefer to eat them this way."

Melanie and Sophie looked exactly like their mother when they pouted. Florian was sure that they'd be just as beautiful as Brigitte had been.

"Can we play Memory afterward?"

"Finally, someone else can take over on Memory duty," said Florian's mother.

"So? How'd you do against the girls?"

"We played five games, and I lost all five."

"I won twice."

"I won three times. Will you play with us?"

"Let your father eat first. He's had a hard day."

"We can start putting the cards out on the table in the living room. Come on, Sophie."

"Thanks," Florian said as his mother served him another pancake.

"I like cooking for you all."

"I mean, thank you for picking the kids up from preschool and taking care of them while I'm at work."

"Please, Florian, you don't have to keep thanking me all the time. I'm happy to do it, and I mean that."

"But it makes things harder for you. And for Dad."

"Oh, he's just a little grumpy sometimes. He loves his granddaughters just as much as I do."

"Have you eaten anything yourself yet?"

"No."

"Then you take the next one."

"Do you want another one?"

"Sure."

"Then you take the next one and then go see the kids. I can wait."

Florian didn't object. He deliberated inwardly for a moment, not actually wanting to know the answer but asking the question anyway: "What happened with the phone? Did she call?"

"I think so."

"What do you mean?"

"The phone rang, and I picked up, but there was no one on the line. Happened three times."

"Judith," concluded Florian.

"Yeah, that's what I thought, too. Obviously, she didn't want to talk to me. I went ahead and disconnected the phone. The constant ringing was getting on my nerves. Should I plug it back in?"

"No, I don't feel like dealing with Judith today, either. I'll play with the kids for a while and then go to bed early. Maybe watch a little TV and fall asleep."

"I don't know what's going on with you and Judith, Florian. But you need to work something out. She's not calming down any. More like she's getting herself worked up about something."

He heard his daughters calling him from the living room. "Daddy! Where are you?"

Sometimes their voices reminded him of his dead wife. If she were still alive, everything would be different.

CHAPTER 30

As Niklas Steg spooned out his alphabet soup, the bright-red locomotive at the bottom of the children's bowl gradually came into view.

"Like it, Nicky?"

"Yes, Mother."

"You see?" Elisabeth Steg turned to look at her husband, Karl. "I told you he'd like it."

Karl rolled his eyes and gave his son a sympathetic look.

"And if you clean your plate, you can have chocolate pudding for dessert."

Nik's phone rang.

"Who's calling you at this hour? If it's Tommy, I already told his mother that you're not allowed to play with him anymore." Nik hadn't seen Tommy in more than thirty years. He couldn't even remember his face.

Roland Thaler was on the other end of the line. He'd been observing Jana Matuschek's apartment for several hours, during which time she'd neither come home nor—now that darkness had fallen—switched any lights on.

Nik got a bad feeling in the pit of his stomach. Something wasn't right here. He ordered two patrolmen over to Jana's apartment before setting off himself. His mother scolded him, but Karl reassured her. She kissed his forehead as he left. Twenty minutes later, he was at Jana's apartment door, along with Thaler and the two other officers.

They rang her doorbell repeatedly, then knocked and shouted that it was the police, that she needed to open the door. They'd break the door down otherwise.

Their entreaties were met with silence.

Realizing that every second might count, Nik ordered a patrolman to kick in the door. Three powerful blows with a boot heel and the door flew open. Nik hurried inside and flipped a light on.

It stank.

Nik recognized the smell, and immediately knew they were too late. He slipped a rubber glove on one hand and then held his nose with the other.

The hallway led past the kitchen, then the bathroom. And there she was, only her head poking out of the water, the tub red with blood. Her eyes were closed peacefully, as though she'd fallen asleep in the bath.

Nik discovered a handwritten note on a stool. The date at the top told him that Jana had been dead for three days. He read the letter without picking it up.

She'd made some mistakes when she was young, it said. Partly the folly of youth, partly because her circumstances had left her little choice. She wished she could turn back time. She was so very, very sorry and ashamed. Her testimony and what she'd told the police was true, she stressed. Schütte was guilty. And she couldn't live with the fact that nobody believed her.

For Detective Niklas Steg, it was the kind of day when he hated his job.

CHAPTER 31
FLASHBACK: THE
FLORIAN LORENZ CASE

Florian Lorenz had a bad feeling about what awaited him. He was only a few minutes late getting home, but Judith needed less than that to make a scene—again. He sensed trouble in the air the moment he opened the door. He removed his shoes and put on slippers before heading to the kitchen, the only room in the apartment with a light on.

"Hello, Judith."

She regarded him silently from her seat at the kitchen table.

Florian took a bottle of apple juice from the refrigerator and drank half of it down in one gulp. He closed his eyes for several seconds. Still not a peep out of Judith. All he wanted to do was relax. He'd been up since six and had worked a long, hard day, tearing down displays at the trade-fair center. A glance at the kitchen clock told him it was past eleven now. *Please don't start with the accusations again,* he thought.

"Sorry I'm a little late."

His partner did not react.

"Why don't we go into the living room and put our feet up?" She didn't move, so he sat down beside her. Her eyes were glittering. "Judith," he said softly, hoping her temper wouldn't flare. He finished the rest of his juice.

"Where were you?" she whispered.

"No, Judith, not this again."

"Where were you?" she repeated.

"Judith, I had a really long day. We were tearing down What about Shoes."

"I called your cell phone at least three times."

"I don't put it in my overalls when I start work. You know that." He pulled the phone out of his pocket and looked at the display: twelve missed calls from Judith Koch. "What were you calling about? Did you want me to pick something up from the store?"

"The store!" she cried scornfully. "And I called the trade-fair stand, too."

"We took out the telephone, along with everything else."

"Then why did I get someone on the line?"

"What do you mean?"

"A coworker of yours answered. Dmitri. He said you were out putting materials in storage."

"I was."

"A minute ago you said they'd disconnected the phone."

"Good grief, Judith. In the afternoon I went out to put stuff in storage, and then one of our last jobs in the evening was to disconnect the phone."

"You're lying to me, Florian. Again."

"Judith." Florian spoke with quiet intensity. "I'm not lying to you."

"Constant excuses, constant fabrications. You don't answer the phone. You say it was off, even though someone picked up. You come home late."

"Less than fifteen minutes late. I can't just drop everything at the end of the day if we're still in the middle of tearing down."

"You were with her again!"

"I don't have a lover, Judith!"

Her accusations rained down on him for the umpteenth time. He was sick of having to explain himself over and over. It had started shortly after they'd met. Whenever he talked to the girl at the bakery counter for longer than was absolutely necessary, whenever a woman eyed him as she walked past, she'd start right in on him. Florian had thought she'd get over her jealousy eventually, but things had only gotten worse.

Suddenly she slammed her fist down onto the table, bouncing the empty glass bottle. Florian flinched.

"Stop lying to me," she screamed, leaping up.

Now Florian was silent. He didn't have the energy to fight this battle yet again.

"Aha. Nothing to say. So I'm right! You were at your bimbo's place while I was here watching your brats."

"There is no bimbo. And don't call my daughters brats."

"They're spoiled, and you know it. Sophie lied to me today. Just like her dear daddy."

"Kids lie sometimes."

"So do adults."

"Judith, I have a hard job, and I have to raise two children by myself. Do you seriously think I have time for a second girlfriend?"

"Apparently you make time. She probably lives near the trade-fair center. That way you can pop over on your lunch break for a quickie. And stupid Judith can stay home and babysit the brats."

"I'm not a brat."

Florian looked toward the door. Melanie was standing there in her nightgown, the one with the moons and unicorns on it, rubbing her eyes.

"Look at that, now you've woken her up."

"Yeah, they're all ahead of me on the list. Your children, your lover, your dead wife."

Inwardly Florian was seething, but he walked calmly over to Melanie and picked her up. "Shh," he said. "It's okay. We were talking a little loudly, that's all. You just go back to bed. I bet you'll be asleep in no time. And we'll be really quiet now."

"But I'm not a brat."

"Of course you aren't, honey." He took Melanie back to bed and tucked her in. When he kissed her on the forehead, she seemed to calm down again and closed her eyes. Soon she was breathing evenly again.

When he returned to the kitchen, Judith had undressed and was leaning provocatively against the kitchen table. "Is this what you want? More sex? What does your bimbo have that I don't?"

"Put your clothes on. Sex is the last thing I want right now."

"Already had enough today, eh?" She came over and caressed his cheek. Then her hand slid down his chest.

"Quit that!" He grabbed her wrist roughly and flung it away.

"You into that? A little rough stuff? Does she let you slap her around and give it to her from behind, your beloved bimbo?"

"Judith, be quiet. The children."

"Yeah, yeah, the children. They remind you so much of your darling Brigitte. The wonderful Brigitte. She could do everything. Mrs. Perfect. Of course, it takes at least two women to replace her."

"Leave Brigitte out of this!"

"She's fighting for you from the grave. Did she like that?"

"Like what?"

"When you got rough."

"I'm telling you for the last time, leave Brigitte out of it!"

Now she turned around and stuck out her backside in his direction. "Come on, take me. Take me the way you took your wife. I bet that's how those two snot-nosed little brats ended up in the world."

"That's it, Judith. You're leaving! Get out of my apartment this instant."

"Aha, now the truth comes out. You want to get rid of me so that your bimbo can move in here."

"You're out of your mind!"

"I'm out of my mind?" Her voice was high and shrill now.

"You should see a therapist. That was some acting job you did those first few weeks."

"Me? I was acting?"

"Get out!"

She stared daggers at him.

"Either you get dressed right now—"

"Or what?"

"Or I'm throwing you out naked." He gripped her forearm, squeezing it tightly.

"Ow!"

"Are you going to leave voluntarily?" Without letting go, he reached out with the other hand and picked up the clothing she had thrown over a kitchen chair. Then he started pulling her away.

"You're hurting me!"

He dragged Judith to the apartment door, opened it, and pushed her out.

She lost her balance and smacked against the banister. Her knee was bleeding, but Florian ignored it. He threw her clothes after her, then fished her keys to his apartment from her handbag and tossed it at her, too, before slamming the door.

She stood there, hammering on the door, screeching the whole time. When a neighbor threatened to call the police, she finally relented.

It took Florian another half hour to get Melanie and Sophie back to sleep again. Then he crawled into bed himself. He didn't know that the horror was only beginning.

CHAPTER 32

Sabrina tapped the "End Call" button on her cell phone and remained motionless at her desk. She didn't know Jana Matuschek or Moritz Schütte, had neither heard the names nor anything about the rape trial. Even so, she was feeling as though she'd eaten something that was well past its expiration date. And this time the folic acid wasn't to blame. She felt dejected and tired. She was aware that Nik's description of Moritz Schütte's murder and the woman's tragic suicide constituted a breach of police confidentiality. She took it as another sign of his trust.

At the time of Moritz Schütte's death, Jana Matuschek was already dead in her bathtub. She couldn't have been the one who killed her rapist. But who had, then? According to Nik, Annika Weiss had an alibi as well. "The third woman" was how Nik put it, and Sabrina was inclined to agree.

Lara's red tomcat, Mielke, rubbed up against her legs and meowed accusingly. Sabrina put out some cat food, then grabbed her purse and headed out. Nik had asked her to speak to Annika Weiss one more time.

If she hadn't been lost in thought, she would have spent a couple of minutes, as she always did, in front of her building, wondering where she'd parked her car. Her short-term memory really did leave a lot to be desired. Today, however, her subconscious took the reins and led her straight to her parking spot.

On her way to Annika Weiss's apartment in Pankow, Sabrina reviewed what she'd learned about the murders. She feared there could soon be even more victims. Mrs. Weiss had to know more than she was telling. Sabrina had to pressure her a little more, as Nik had suggested. Her chances with Dominik Weiss's widow were better than the police's. In an official interrogation, Annika Weiss would probably exercise her right to remain silent immediately.

Sabrina had to ring the doorbell three times before Mrs. Weiss buzzed her in. She didn't seem pleased to see Sabrina. After an awkward moment at the door, she led Sabrina into the living room. "Well? How's your stomach?"

"What do you mean?"

"Last time you were here, you'd had too many mojitos the night before."

Not wanting to go into detail about folic acid, Sabrina didn't contradict her. Annika Weiss didn't offer her anything to drink this time. She looked uncomfortable in Sabrina's presence but didn't seem able to distance herself. Presumably, she'd had the same problem when it came to her sadistic husband.

"Physically I'm doing great today," Sabrina replied.

Her choice of words was not lost on Mrs. Weiss, who raised one eyebrow. "Physically?"

Sabrina needed a way to draw the other woman out. "Two more people have died," she said.

Annika Weiss flinched, and Sabrina could see that she hadn't heard anything about them.

"A young woman is dead. Suicide. She was raped a couple of weeks ago in Tiergarten. And the perpetrator was found dead later on as well." Sabrina told her about the trial, and how it had ended in an acquittal.

"And what does that have to do with me?"

"All the signs point to him having been murdered by the same person who was responsible for your husband's death."

Annika Weiss pursed her lips.

"He was, in a matter of speaking, executed. Just like your husband. And the words *reap the storm* were written in blood on the wall, just like in your apartment."

"I had nothing to do with that."

"Mrs. Weiss, your husband was shot. A few days later, you get caught holding the murder weapon, using it to threaten a convicted sex offender. And then a couple of days later, another man, presumably a rapist, is killed the same way your husband was. And you claim you had nothing to do with any of it?"

"I didn't kill my husband or that rapist. But it served him right. Why didn't they find him guilty?"

"Served him right? Did it serve your husband right as well?"

The room was silent for a moment. Sabrina glanced around the room. The Bible was no longer lying on the chest of drawers. "You were looking something up in the Old Testament last time I was here."

Annika Weiss started but remained silent.

"For they have sown wind and shall reap the whirlwind," Sabrina quoted. "Someone is after revenge here, not justice. Did your husband sexually assault you, Mrs. Weiss?"

The woman's expression told Sabrina she'd guessed correctly.

"This third woman—yes, they've already proven that it's a woman—helped you get revenge on your husband. And she committed at least one other murder, and incited you to one as well."

Annika Weiss couldn't bear the weight of Sabrina's gaze any longer; stricken, she looked down at the floor.

"That's taking the law into your own hands, Mrs. Weiss. You know that. And you know that you're very much involved here." Sabrina waited to see if Annika had anything to say in response. "Attempted murder," she went on. "Conspiracy to commit murder. Solicitation to murder. Any of those could get you life in prison, Mrs. Weiss."

"I didn't know that Schütte guy at all," she replied meekly.

"That doesn't matter. You know the perpetrator. And if you don't tell me or the police who she is, you could face charges for every additional murder she commits. Or do you think she's going to just quit?"

Annika Weiss pondered her circumstances. She had difficulty looking Sabrina in the eye. "She called me, and we met at a park in Pankow. She knew about my problems with Dominik."

"Tell me the whole story."

And the more Annika Weiss spoke, the more certain Sabrina was that something about her seemed familiar. But what it was, she still couldn't put her finger on.

CHAPTER 33

FLASHBACK: THE DOMINIK WEISS CASE

Three thirty p.m., Pankow Public Park. That was the time and location Annika Weiss had agreed upon with the unknown caller. She knew Dominik was still at work. He wouldn't be home in time to start questioning her about why she'd gone out. Not this time. She resolved to be home within an hour. She'd learned only too well that it was better to avoid unnecessary questions. Her husband was seldom satisfied with the answers she gave. He always found a way to put her down, intimidate her. He would argue and maneuver until she was too exhausted to keep defending herself, which he always interpreted as an admission that he was right.

The "victories" often ended in violence. And that excited him even more. He would grab her, throw her on the bed, tie her wrists and ankles to the bed frame, and take what he considered rightfully his. The brutality had increased over the years.

The woman who had called Annika knew about Dominik's vicious attacks. But how?

Annika stopped in front of the memorial to the Czechoslovakian resistance fighter Julius Fučik and read the inscription: "Mankind, I loved you. Be vigilant!"

Yes, she'd loved Dominik once, too. His confident, masculine presence. That he knew what he wanted and found a way to get it. She hadn't realized it would extend to her as well, that he considered her his property, to do with as he pleased. By the time she did fully realize it, it was too late. She was unable to break free of his spell. Not by herself. The stranger had promised to help her.

Annika Weiss looked around, searching. She had no idea what the woman looked like, but the woman had assured her she would recognize Annika.

There she was. Coming up the path, straight toward her. It had to be her. About her age, thirtyish, Annika guessed. Short brown hair, lots of makeup, light-blue business suit—she could have been a bank teller.

When she spotted Annika, she smiled briefly before her face grew serious again. "Hello, Mrs. Weiss. I'm very glad you came."

Annika nodded.

"Is it okay if I call you Annika?" Without waiting for a reply, she introduced herself as Jennifer.

Annika doubted that it was her real name.

"Shall we walk a little?"

"Okay," Annika said, feeling uncertain and subdued.

"It's always hard to talk about," Jennifer began quietly. "I've spoken to so many women about it. And I know from personal experience how you feel." Her voice was gentle and understanding. Annika felt herself beginning to trust her. "My mother was raped by her husband as well."

Rape. Annika had never spoken the word aloud herself. In the first few years of her marriage, when she'd confided in her girlfriends, she consistently downplayed her husband's attacks. If that upsetting word came up, she always objected. No, Dominik wasn't a bad person. She must have done something wrong.

She'd lost touch with all her girlfriends years ago. She was alone with her pain.

"I'm here with you, Annika." Jennifer stopped and took her hand. Then she turned Annika toward her so she could look into her eyes. "I'm here with you," she repeated, "and I'm going to help you."

Annika swallowed.

"I used to want to study psychology. But I found it very difficult to maintain professional distance from other people's problems. Now I'm better at it." They started walking again. "It's my father's fault, my fate. And it was my mother's fate, too."

"What happened?"

"She killed herself when I was still in elementary school. I was the one who found her."

"How horrible!" Just imagining it made Annika's stomach turn.

"My father was a pig. And he drove my mother to her death. He raped her. Over and over again. I lay there in my bed, hearing her scream."

"Why didn't she leave him?"

"Why don't you leave your husband, Annika?"

But the question was rhetorical. Jennifer knew the answer: Annika didn't have the strength to leave her husband and break the cycle of violence.

"It was the same for my mother. Plus she had a small child." Now Jennifer was having trouble continuing as well. "He said that if she left him, he'd find us. And that everything would get worse, much worse."

An older couple walked past, and the two women lapsed into silence until they were out of hearing range.

"She stayed with him because of me. I carried that guilt around for years."

"But you were just a child. There was nothing you could have done."

"I understand that now."

"Even without a child, perhaps she wouldn't have had the strength. Like me."

Jennifer neither agreed nor disagreed. "Shall we sit down?" She pointed to a park bench. It faced the Panke River, which flowed quietly toward the inner harbor where it met the Spree. A mother duck swam past with five ducklings in single file behind her.

"Later on I ended up with foster parents."

"And things were okay with them?" Annika wanted to know.

"More or less."

To Annika it sounded like Jennifer had never come to terms with her childhood.

"Someone just has to get rid of him," said Jennifer.

"Who?"

"The man."

"What do you mean by 'get rid of him'?"

"I mean it the way I said it."

One of the ducklings veered off on its own, but eventually its mother's agitated quacking led it back to its siblings.

"I can't stand the fact that pigs like those are allowed to keep on living," Jennifer went on.

Annika couldn't count the number of times she'd wished Dominik were dead over the years. And she'd always been ashamed of herself for it. Now, after sitting for a while, she could feel her injuries from the previous night, and for the first time, she began to view the idea in a positive light.

"I saw him."

"My husband?"

"No, my father. After all those years."

"What did he say?"

"I don't think he recognized me." Then, sarcastically, she added, "Maybe if I'd taken my clothes off."

"Isn't he in jail?"

"He was, yeah. But now he's back out on the streets."

Annika noticed that Jennifer was trembling.

"I don't think he was sufficiently punished. My mother is still dead. And I'll be suffering for the rest of my life." Her voice was bitter, but quiet and even. "Now he's a member of society in good standing again. Until he goes after his next victim."

"Maybe he's changed," Annika said.

"Once a pig, always a pig," Jennifer replied. "Or has your husband gotten better in recent years?"

The opposite was the case, and both women knew it.

Jennifer glanced surreptitiously in every direction to make sure they weren't being watched. Then she opened up her purse and pulled out a pistol.

Annika started.

"I bought it in Hasenheide, no questions asked. It's a relic from the Soviet era. There are still hundreds of them all over the former East Germany."

"I've never held a gun before."

"I'll show you." With practiced movements, she held the pistol out and wrapped her free hand around her trigger hand to stabilize it. Then she aimed at the mother duck and showed Annika how to remove the safety catch. "And then all you have to do is pull the trigger. And don't let it scare you. The recoil will knock your hand upward."

"Why are you telling me this?"

"I want you to kill my father." Coolly she stuck the pistol back into her purse.

"Excuse me?"

"I'll get rid of your husband, and you kill my father in exchange. Death is the only just punishment for rape."

Annika was appalled. The very idea frightened her. "No," she said. "Never. I could never kill another person."

"You're not killing a person. You're killing a pig. The world will be a better place without your husband and without my father."

Annika started to rise, but Jennifer grabbed her arm. "Don't worry. Nothing will happen to us. Neither of us has motives, and we'll make sure we have alibis. Nothing can go wrong."

"No," Annika repeated, removing Jennifer's hand from her forearm.

"You already know this is the answer to all your problems."

Annika didn't want to hear it. She strode rapidly away from the park bench.

"You have my number," Jennifer called after her. "Call me once you've thought it over."

What frightened Annika the most was that she'd already played the scenario out in her mind, and deep inside she knew that she really would prefer Dominik dead. She was more afraid of herself than of Jennifer.

"You already know this is the answer to all your problems." The words echoed in her mind.

And suddenly her intuition told her who the woman actually was. She pushed the thought aside. And she didn't mention it when she told Sabrina Lampe about the fateful meeting in Pankow Public Park, the day it all began.

CHAPTER 34

Florian Lorenz had an uneasy feeling in the pit of his stomach. His boss, Karl-Heinz Wolters, had asked to speak to him. Now, standing in front of Wolters's office door, his discomfort intensified. He knocked tentatively. "Come in," came the reply.

The head of the trade-fair construction company welcomed him and gestured to the small seating area in the corner of his office. Florian could detect no warmth in Wolters's expression. Had he done something wrong? Filled out an order incorrectly?

Late for work once too often? Whatever it was, Wolters's demeanor was solemn.

Florian sat down. Wolters offered him a glass of water, but Florian politely declined it.

He'd taken the liberty of leaving early the day before. His coworkers told him it was okay with them. They knew he was a single father and were understanding of his situation. Did Wolters have a problem with that? He'd never objected in the past.

Florian waited for the other man to initiate the conversation.

"Are you having personal problems, Mr. Lorenz?"

"What do you mean?"

"I know you went through some hard times." He lowered his voice. "The death of your wife. Not something a person can work through in just two years. And then working full-time and taking care of two small children, that really commands my respect."

Florian wasn't sure what Wolters was getting at.

"We're all behind you, Mr. Lorenz. Everyone here knows what an honest, hardworking person you are. And of course we remember what a fun-loving guy you were before your wife got sick."

Brigitte appeared in his mind. The way she had been before the diagnosis. She'd changed so rapidly afterward, practically wilted and dissolved before his eyes. In six months, she was a shadow of her old self. In the end, death had come as a release, the pain and her suffering at an end.

"Mr. Lorenz?"

Wolters's voice jolted him out of his painful memories.

"It's nearly impossible to replace a loved one with someone else, I suppose."

What was he talking about? Shouldn't they be discussing work?

"Your new girlfriend called."

Judith! Florian started.

Wolters had nearly stumbled on the word *girlfriend*.

"We broke up."

"Excellent decision," Wolters said.

But Florian didn't think he'd ever met Judith.

"She didn't call just once. She dialed your colleague Mr. Kudraczek, Mrs. Sommergerst in the HR department, and even me."

Florian reddened with shame. *Goddamn Judith!* He didn't know what had driven him into her arms in the first place. Grief? The way her eyes had reminded him of Brigitte's? A moment of weakness?

"I'm very sorry, Mr. Wolters. I had no idea. This is very upsetting, to me as well. I'll go right over and apologize to Mrs. Sommergerst. And to Dmitri."

"That's not why I called you in here."

Florian didn't understand.

"That woman is dangerous. She insulted you in despicable terms. Your children, too."

Brigitte as well, I'm sure, thought Florian. *Wolters is just too considerate to mention that.*

"She's spreading rumors that you raped her repeatedly."

Florian was looking down dejectedly, but he could feel Wolters's querying eyes on him. "She's lying," he said quietly.

"That's all I wanted to hear, Mr. Lorenz. I believe you. With the way this woman is behaving, there's only one conclusion I can draw. She wants to frame you."

"Thank you," Florian whispered without looking his supervisor in the eye.

"Mrs. Sommergerst was very discreet about the whole thing. She doesn't gossip. She came straight to me. All of us here are on your side. But unfortunately, I can't guarantee this won't have broader repercussions."

After all the grieving over his wife, he'd gone and landed himself a psychopath.

"Have you considered going to the police about this?"

The thought hadn't even crossed his mind.

"This is stalking, Mr. Lorenz. I urge you to be proactive. I'm afraid this woman will go on making your life hell. And eventually she'll make something stick."

Florian Lorenz felt utterly despondent. When they concluded their conversation, he extended a limp hand, but his boss shook it firmly and warmly.

"Go home. Mr. Kudraczek and the others will manage without you today. Get some rest. Play with your children."

Florian managed a grateful nod.

He was practically in a trance on the way home. What to do about Judith? Should he actually go to the police? Really bring out the big guns like that? Surely Judith would calm down again eventually. Maybe he should just ignore her. If he didn't react, she'd lose interest in time, wouldn't she?

His apartment door told him otherwise. The entire surface was covered in scratches. Someone had gone at it with a knife. There was no question in Florian's mind who that someone was. The word *pig* was carved in capital letters at eye level. And she'd tried her luck with the lock, too. Without success, fortunately.

With a long sigh, Florian realized he was bone weary. He couldn't take it anymore.

The police, yeah, maybe Wolters was right. Maybe he really did need to go to the police. But first he just wanted to sit down and put his feet up for a few minutes.

He fell asleep almost immediately. Didn't wake up until his mother brought his daughters home from preschool.

"What's this?" she asked, holding up the postcard that he'd brought in with the mail the day before and put down somewhere without thinking about it. "Sow the wind . . . ," she read aloud as the girls first kissed their father and then ran off to their room.

Florian only shrugged. He couldn't worry about that on top of everything else. He took the postcard and threw it in the trash.

CHAPTER 35

FLASHBACK: THE DOMINIK WEISS CASE

It took Annika Weiss less than a week to decide if she would meet Jennifer again. Her husband had provided forceful assistance with the decision-making process, in the most literal sense.

Like so many times before, she'd gone to bed before him, hoping to be asleep by the time he joined her. He usually left her alone then. She awoke to slaps to her face; her right ear began to ring. She wanted to defend herself, to shout at him, but his paw was clamped down over her mouth. So viciously that now her jaw hurt as well.

"Are you going to be good or what?"

The bit of air she managed to inhale through her nose gave her just enough strength to nod. When she resisted, it only excited him all the more. She kept still.

Kept still as he tied her wrists and ankles into place.

Kept still as he blindfolded her.

Kept still as he gagged her.

She was helpless, and she could sense how much it turned him on. She cried, she tried to scream. She tried to picture herself somewhere else, anywhere. But what lay in store for her was worse than ever before. He'd gotten a new "toy." Mercilessly, he forced it in. Pain exploded throughout her abdomen. Then she blacked out.

When she woke up the next morning, she was thankful to be alive. Her bruised arms and legs ached. She felt like what she imagined a rugby player must feel like after a grueling match. Her ear was still ringing. But all of that was nothing compared to the unrelenting pain between her legs. Thank God he'd left the house.

With great effort she managed to change the blood-drenched sheets. Then she retrieved the scrap of paper with the phone number on it from its hiding place behind the cans in the pantry. She stared at it for several seconds, until the numbers began to blur. When she managed to bring them into focus again, she dialed the number quickly, before she could change her mind.

It took her twice as long to get to Pankow Public Park as it had the first time. Sitting down on the bench wasn't an option; as soon as she started to squat, the pain became unbearable. She hoped she had taken sufficient precautions to keep any blood from seeping through.

Jennifer didn't keep her waiting long.

Annika hadn't told her on the phone why she'd changed her mind. But Jennifer discerned immediately from Annika's pained expression and limited range of motion. Jennifer drew her into her arms and hugged her gently, making sure not to cause her any additional pain. Annika began to cry. Tears that she had suppressed for so long, not wanting to acknowledge her situation, spilled down her cheeks at last.

Agreeing on a day and a course of action was merely a formality.

Jennifer held up her end of the bargain. She gave Dominik Weiss what, as far as she was concerned, he deserved. She also did it for her mother, who had died so long ago. And she smiled in satisfaction at the knowledge that her father, Gerd Lucke, would soon share Dominik Weiss's fate.

CHAPTER 36

"This can't go on, Florian. You're pale and tense. Your hands are shaking." His mother untied her apron in one swift motion.

Florian Lorenz knew that she was right. He laid his left hand on the kitchen table and told himself to relax. He'd pulled himself together while he was putting Melanie and Sophie to bed. But now that his daughters had fallen asleep, the worrying had started again, and he couldn't hide it any longer. His fingers continued to twitch, refusing to obey him.

"She's started talking to me on the phone now."

Florian wanted to put his hands over his ears and not hear anything else about Judith.

Instead, he murmured a barely audible "What does she say?"

His mother sat down next to him and laid her hands on both of his, quieting them. Florian sighed. "First I want you to know that we'll stand by you no matter what happens."

As an introductory sentence, Florian thought, it didn't sound particularly promising.

"I spent a long time talking this over with your father. He agrees with me one hundred percent."

What was she talking about? He gave her a questioning look.

"Until now, she always hung up whenever I answered your phone. Today she called us at home. Your father picked up."

"And?"

"You know your father. His whole face turned red. Thank goodness he's started taking those blood pressure pills."

"What did she want?"

"To say terrible things about you, of course."

Florian closed his eyes. What had he done to deserve this? His mother lowered her voice, as though someone might hear them. "She told Dad that you had mistreated her and . . ." She couldn't finish, but Florian knew how the sentence would have ended.

"Please, Florian. Obviously, we don't believe a word of what she said. Your father didn't take her seriously for one second, either." His mother was silent for a moment. "She called Bertha, too."

"Aunt Bertha? What does she have to do with any of this? Judith only met her once in her life, at Dad's birthday party." Every time Florian thought things couldn't get any worse, reality contradicted him.

"No idea. But you know Bertha. She called me immediately, and after that probably all of our other relatives."

What an utter disaster. Florian knew right away that his boss had been right: with accusations like these, something would eventually stick, true or not.

"Then your father told me he saw her at the grocery store. She'd been watching him shop."

"What? At the store near you guys?"

"The day before yesterday. He hadn't told me because he didn't want to upset me."

"She doesn't live anywhere near you two."

"Your father and I suspect that she's trying to find out who we talk to."

"I don't understand."

"For her it's not enough to turn your friends and coworkers against you. Now she's thinking bigger."

"She's sick."

"Yes, but knowing that doesn't help you."

Of course his mother was right. Mental illness was an explanation, but not an excuse. And the fact that Judith was sick wasn't going to help him solve the problem.

"She'll keep doing this, Florian."

He nodded.

"You have to meet up with her, try to talk some sense into her."

"What!"

"She won't stop this on her own."

"But I couldn't sit down at the same table with her now. Not after all the lies she's been spreading about me."

"You could always go to the police."

"Slander. Stalking."

"Right. But my guess is that if you do that, then she'll really start in on you. She'll defend herself. It'll be your word against hers. She won't give up, Florian."

"So I should apologize to her?" Florian was incredulous.

"You should explain to her one more time why the relationship has to end. She needs to understand your perspective."

"You know, I tried telling her many times that we just don't belong together. I tried to break it to her gently. But it didn't work, so I started being more blunt."

He was beginning to see that he had no choice. He had to bite the bullet and meet Judith one more time.

"If that doesn't work," his mother said, "you can always go to the police later."

CHAPTER 37

Café Victoria was close to the Victory Column. Florian Lorenz had driven by it plenty of times, but he'd never been inside. He looked around. Most of the guests were probably tourists who'd come to this part of Tiergarten to see the monument and were fortifying themselves with coffee and cake before or after the arduous climb up to the observation deck.

No sign of Judith yet. She'd chosen the café; Florian hadn't cared one way or the other. Getting together with her was awful enough—the choice of location didn't make a difference.

Florian took the only free table he saw and ordered a glass of water. His nerves were already shot—coffee would only make it worse. He sat still and concentrated on his breathing, hoping to keep himself calm.

Judith kept him waiting for another ten minutes before marching in, head held high, with a triumphant smile on her face. When she sat down across from him, she didn't say a word. She waited until Florian had forced out a quiet hello and merely nodded.

The waitress appeared, and Judith ordered a latte macchiato and a piece of chocolate cheesecake.

"How lovely of you to invite me out on this date, my darling Florian." She gave him a challenging smile.

Those words alone were enough to destroy Florian's good intentions. "This isn't a *date*, and you know it, Judith. And I am definitely not your darling Florian."

For a moment her facade seemed to slip, but she recovered and started right in again. "Oh, don't make such a fuss now. You didn't want to go to our favorite café, where we spent so many lovely afternoons."

Although he'd left the choice of location up to her, he'd expressly requested that it be somewhere neutral. He didn't want to go over the reasons for that again, not here. "Cut it out. You know exactly why we're here."

"Because of all the wonderful times we had together? Because things ought to go back to how they were before? Because you've finally come to your senses?"

"Me? I've come to my senses?" He laughed out loud. The guests at the neighboring tables turned to look at him. He lowered his voice. "I want this to stop."

"You want what to stop?"

"You know exactly what I'm talking about." The word *bitch* nearly slipped out at the end, but he managed to get himself under control.

She blinked seductively. Only now did he notice how dolled up she was. Did she actually believe she could win him back? After everything that had happened?

Her hand slid over the table to the hand he was gripping his water glass in. Hastily he let go of the glass and jerked his hand away. What had he ever seen in this woman?

She'd deceived him at the beginning of their relationship. Acted loving, sensitive, understanding. Now he knew that it had all been one big charade. Playing a role, pretending to be someone else, that only worked for a while. Sooner or later, the web of deceit always fell apart.

Unfortunately for Florian, he hadn't seen through her until it was too late.

"Have you given it some more thought?" Judith asked sweetly.

What could she possibly mean?

"Your situation. Your kids and so on."

"I don't understand."

"Well, I mean, I really do think your girlfriend ought to be the number-one priority in your life. I'm sure we'll find a solution for your daughters. Maybe we can just ship them off to your mother's. Or find an affordable boarding school."

"You can't actually be serious."

"Obviously you'll have to quit this nonsense with other women, too. We don't want even more little brats showing up."

"Are you out of your mind?"

"Not so loud, Florian, darling. People are looking at us again."

"I'm not your darling," he said loudly, not caring about the other guests.

"Screaming at me isn't very constructive." Judith was astonishingly calm. Florian feared her behavior was part of a larger scheme. "I'm quite sure some of the people here will remember this temper tantrum of yours if anyone questions them. Poor, poor Judith sitting across from him, quiet and innocent."

Florian felt the blood rushing to his head. His mind somersaulted. It was as if he had left his body and was watching himself from the outside. He'd never experienced anything like it. Under the table, his hands balled into fists.

Looking perfectly relaxed, Judith reached for her latte macchiato, slurped it with visible enjoyment, and set it on the table again. "That's how it was when you raped me, too."

"What?"

"You sexually assaulted me three times. Always after your brats were already in bed. You put your hand over my mouth so I wouldn't wake them up. I flailed around, tried to defend myself, but you were just stronger than me."

Florian felt his fingernails digging into his palms. "You know perfectly well that's not true."

"But of course it's true." She told the lie with an absolutely straight face. "And soon I'll have everyone else convinced, too. Your mother. Your friends. Your boss."

He got a strong impression that she had even come to believe the story herself. "Stop this, Judith," he said very quietly one last time.

She ignored the request. "The district attorney. The jury. The judge."

His control gave way to rage. Slamming his fists on the table, he leaped up and lunged at her. Judith barely managed to scoot her chair back before Florian's hands could close around her neck. He was about to try again, but found himself being forcibly restrained.

"Careful!" Judith screamed. "He probably has a knife!" Hurriedly she rolled up her sleeve. "Look, this is where he cut me." There was a gash on the underside of her arm that had just begun to heal.

"You goddamn—"

That was as far as he got. "You're out of here, mister!" one of the men holding him shouted. He continued his efforts to break free and attack Judith as the two men dragged him out and threw him to the ground in front of the café entrance.

"Now get lost before we have to hurt you!"

Florian picked himself up with a look toward the entrance, the men, arms crossed, barring his way. He turned and ran off, adrenaline coursing through him, in the direction of Tiergarten. He kept on running, he didn't know how long. When he came to a park bench, he sat down.

He could still picture the sneering grin on Judith's face when he lost it—presumably exactly the way she'd hoped.

He had no choice but to try plan B. He decided not to put it off any longer. After asking a passerby where the nearest police station was, he went in and filed a report.

He was starting to fear that Judith would do the same.

CHAPTER 38

INTERLUDE: *NIGHT TALK*,
101.1 RADIO SPREE ANTENNA

"So the weather will be about the same as today. Oh, well. But here at 101.1 Radio Spree Antenna, the skies are always clear, my dear listeners. It's twelve past twelve, and it's that time—*Night Talk* with the She-Wolf."

(Jingle.)

"My name is Franziska Lupa, and I hope you're having a wonderful evening. If not, call me. Hello?"

"Good evening. My name is Judith."

"That's not your real name."

"Yes, it is. I have nothing to hide."

(Silence.)

"What's on your mind, Judith?"

"It's about my partner."

"Please don't use any real names, all right? Let's call him . . . Michael."

"He can't get over his ex-wife."

"He's divorced?"

"No, she died."

"So you're in competition with his deceased wife?"

"Yeah, exactly. And his children are always conspiring against me."

"How many children? How old?"

"Two girls. Around six."

"You don't know exactly?"

"No idea."

"Maybe if you show more interest in the children, they'll accept you more."

"It's not about me, it's about—"

"Michael."

"And the brats totally cling to him. He spends more time with them than he does with me."

"Children that age need their father, even more so if their mother's no longer around."

"And he's cheating on me."

"Are you sure?"

"Of course. He's constantly working overtime, or else he has to take care of his brats. That's when he's with her. It might even be several different women."

"Do you have proof?"

"Proof? I don't need proof. He's sex obsessed, driven by his physical urges."

"What makes you think that?"

(Silence.)

"He raped me multiple times."

(Silence.)

"Those are serious accusations."

"They aren't accusations. They're facts."

"You have to go to the police about this, Judith."

"I already did. They don't believe me. They think I'm the guilty one."

"That happens a lot, unfortunately. Rapists get acquitted. For lack of evidence. Or because the woman shouldn't have been wearing such sexy clothes. But the police should know better."

"But they're not doing anything about it. They just let him keep doing as he pleases."

"What do you mean?"

"I'm really afraid for the two girls. He's probably alone with them in the apartment as we speak."

CHAPTER 39

Nearly a week had gone by since Moritz Schütte's murder. The police investigation hadn't made much progress. The members of the newly established special investigative team were meeting in Chief Detective Zimmermann's office. Roland Thaler was asked to summarize the facts of the case and their current theories.

"Two women, Annika Weiss and another we don't know, meet up and agree that they'll each commit a murder. Crisscross, so to speak. The unknown woman commits her crime. Annika Weiss fails. One of our two victims is Dominik Weiss, who likely assaulted his wife sexually on a regular basis. Statements by neighbors and by Mrs. Weiss's doctor support that statement. Why they didn't react sooner is another question. The other victim is a rapist as well. He, however, committed his crime more than twenty years ago, and already served his sentence."

"Question," Zimmermann broke in, shifting his body mass in his too-small office chair. "Have we learned who was involved in that case yet?"

"We're working on it," Jasmin Ibscher replied. "So far we haven't found any commonalities—not among the witnesses, the officers, or the attorneys involved."

"What about the girl, Gerd Lucke's daughter?"

"Still working on that, too," Jasmin said. "We've requested the complete files from the district court, the juvenile dependency court, and Child Protective Services. It's been slow going because the child was given a new name at the time of adoption, and they didn't keep electronic archives back then. And personal information is kept strictly confidential in those types of cases for the child's protection. But we made sure they know how important and how urgent this inquiry is."

"Thank you. Go on, Thaler."

"In each case, the intended victim was first sent a postcard with the words *sow the wind* written on it. Moritz Schütte received such a postcard as well, shortly before he was killed. The murder weapon in that case was also a Makarov. Those are still circulating around the former East Germany, leftover Soviet stock. Our perpetrator seems to have found a source for those. Schütte was charged with rape, but his lawyer got him acquitted."

"So this woman is acting as a kind of angel of vengeance, and rapists are her target," Nik concluded. "Her brand of vigilantism is meticulously planned and exceptionally gruesome. And she is unconcerned with leaving DNA or fingerprints at the crime scene."

"That type of killer often wants to be found out eventually," Zimmermann remarked.

"True," Nik agreed. "She probably sees herself as a kind of hero, a role model for rape victims. You see, the government can't protect us, she reasons, so we have to take matters into our own hands."

Jasmin put it more bluntly: "Join me, sisters. Let's kill these rapist pigs!"

A moment of silence followed.

"We haven't gotten anywhere with the Makarovs," Emma Dombrowski spoke up. "We tracked down an illegal weapons dealer, but we're certain he has nothing to do with the case. We've seized quite a few weapons, but none of them were Soviet made. Anyway, the weapons dealer has been out of the country for several weeks."

"At least that's an interim victory," grunted Zimmermann. "A bone we can throw the press."

"Speaking of press," Nik said. Zimmermann gave him a questioning look. "I think it's time we take the case public. A few journalists have already begun to suspect connections between the Dominik Weiss and Moritz Schütte murders. Word of Jana Matuschek's suicide has gotten out as well. We should grab the bull by the horns before the press starts throwing around a bunch of half-baked theories."

"Whoever she is," added Jasmin, "she's not going to stop. Serial killers seldom do. And with the success she's had so far, she's probably even more motivated."

"But if we put out a press release," Thaler said, "wouldn't that practically encourage her to keep going?"

"We'll have to take that risk," Nik replied. "Protecting the next potential victim has to take priority. Unless our dubious Lady Vengeance decides to change her behavior pattern, somebody else will be getting a postcard, or has gotten one already. And he should understand the seriousness of it and come to us."

"That's what we'll do," Zimmermann declared, already fishing a pack of cigarettes out of his drawer, which was the signal to his employees that the discussion was over. "I want the text for the press release on my desk in an hour." Without waiting for the others to leave the office, he lit a cigarette.

CHAPTER 40

Florian Lorenz had been meaning to cancel his *Berliner Morgenpost* subscription for a while. He rarely found time to read the newspaper anymore. Sometimes he flipped through it listlessly in the morning and skimmed the headlines; other times, the paper landed in the recycling bin unread.

His mother had already picked up his daughters to take them to preschool, and it was mere coincidence that his gaze fell upon the three words at the top of an article in today's paper. A shiver ran down his back when he made the connection—the exact words on the postcard he'd found in his mailbox a few days before: "Sow the Wind . . ." Curiosity piqued, he read the rest of the article, and his agitation increased. Two men had been murdered after receiving such a postcard, with an attempt on a third. He rubbed his eyes and read the lines over again.

Was this actually happening to him? He felt like he was watching a movie or reading a book. His stomach turned with the realization that he was playing one of the main parts.

But why? Why him, of all people? The article was talking about sexual assault. About revenge on rapists. What did that have to do with him?

Forgetting it was time to leave for work, he dialed the number listed under the article. A Detective Niklas Steg answered the phone, and not thirty minutes later, the man was sitting at his kitchen table, along with a female officer whose name Florian had forgotten.

Afterward, everything that happened from that point on felt almost dreamlike. He remembered calling his boss to ask for the day off. The two detectives looking awfully worried. Plastic-glove-clad hands fishing the ominous postcard out of his trashcan.

Thanks to the police report he'd filed the day before, the detectives already knew about Judith Koch. He told them more.

About his wife's early death from cancer. About his children. And all about his involvement with Judith—a promising start that had quickly turned into a living nightmare.

And when he saw the look of alarm on the detectives' faces as he was telling them about the rape accusations, it all fell into place. There it was, the connection to the newspaper article. Florian knew immediately that he was in serious danger.

Steg made a phone call; the words *police protection* came up. When a uniformed officer showed up at Florian's apartment shortly afterward, Steg made sure he had taken down Judith Koch's address correctly, and then he and the female detective left.

And only then did Florian's mind stop spinning enough that he could start processing what had just happened.

CHAPTER 41

In his twenty years on the force, Nik had become a good judge of people. As a rule, he could tell whether the person he was talking to was being genuine or putting on an act.

From the start of the interview with Judith Koch, she smiled charmingly, made sure he saw her best side. Several times he got the feeling she was flirting with him. The way she batted her eyelashes or subtly displayed her feminine charms left little doubt there. But he didn't trust her. His gut told him something was off. Sitting across from her, it was plain to see that she usually got what she wanted from men, with her long blonde hair, model-thin figure, short skirt, long legs.

A lot of men probably fell for it. Nik probed beneath the surface glamour. He noticed that Jasmin was studying him. No doubt she recognized the Koch woman's wiles and was probably checking on Nik to make sure he wasn't buying any of it.

It was clear to him how this woman had managed to wrap Florian Lorenz around her little finger. Lorenz had seemed like a perfectly nice guy to Nik. He also understood that Lorenz's thick brown hair, muscular torso, and masculine looks greatly appealed to the ladies. He wasn't surprised Ms. Koch had wanted to get her claws into him. Lorenz, lonely and weakened by the loss of his wife, had been easy prey for a woman like Judith Koch.

He hadn't seen what she was really like until later.

Later, but hopefully not too late.

"I have no idea why Mr. Lorenz filed these charges against me."

"He said you were constantly calling him. His house, his mother's house, his place of work."

"*Constantly* is an exaggeration. Sure, I tried to reach him once or twice. But isn't that normal when someone leaves you? Just like that? Out of the blue? A person wants to know why. Wouldn't you want to know why, Mr. Steg?"

Nik ignored the question. "According to Mr. Lorenz, you've called several times a day for the past two weeks. He told us it was thirty or forty calls."

"Oh, he's exaggerating, Mr. Steg." Nik saw that Judith Koch was largely ignoring Jasmin. He was the man, and he was higher ranked. Judith was focusing on the person whose support would be most advantageous for her.

"We can have your phone records checked. Then we'll know how often you called."

It wouldn't actually have been quite that easy, but she fell for his bluff. "All right, it was more than once or twice. But you have to understand, I was in complete despair." Was she trying to squeeze out a tear? "He just threw me out. For no reason. And without a word of explanation. I think any woman would want to find out what was going on."

Now she sought out Jasmin's eyes and wiped an imaginary tear from her cheek, smearing her makeup. Jasmin's expression remained alert and emotionless. Failing to win her sympathy, Judith turned her attention back to Nik.

"Ms. Koch, are you familiar with the Old Testament?" he asked.

"No. I grew up in East Germany, as it was known then. Religious instruction was frowned on."

Nik laid a copy of the postcard they'd found at Dominik Weiss's apartment on the table.

"Sow the wind . . . ," the suspect read aloud. "Oh, is that a Bible quote? I thought that was from some movie. How does it end again? Reap the storm?"

She seemed genuinely surprised—or was it another act? Nik wasn't sure this time. "Have you ever seen this postcard before?"

"No." The answer came quickly.

"Would you mind if we fingerprint you and check that?"

"Go ahead," she said, holding out her hand as though she expected him to kiss it.

"Thank you. After we're through here, we'll send you down to our colleague in forensics, and she'll take care of it."

"Am I under arrest now, Detective?"

All this batting of eyes was getting on his nerves.

"As we stated at the beginning," Jasmin spoke up, "you're here of your own free will. You're free to get up and leave whenever you like."

"I have nothing to hide," she said, not taking her eyes off Nik. "Naturally, I'll be happy to work with the police to clear up this misunderstanding."

"In fact, this is about more than Mr. Lorenz's police report."

"What do you mean?"

He told her the date and time of Dominik Weiss's murder. "Where were you then?"

Unflustered, she pulled a phone out of her bright-red purse and flipped it open with one pointed fingernail. "Let's see." She swiped back and forth across the display. "I was at the office."

"That late on a Friday evening?"

"I work in a call center. It's open around the clock."

"Can anyone confirm that?"

"Of course. I work in an open-plan office. On Friday evenings there are always at least a dozen other people there."

Nik didn't let his disappointment show. "Does the name Jana Matuschek mean anything to you?"

"No."

"Moritz Schütte?"

"No."

He named Schütte's time of death as well.

Judith flipped through her phone again. "I was out shopping with my best friend. Do you want her number?"

He nodded, and Jasmin wrote it down. "I think that's all for now, Ms. Koch. You don't have any travel plans in the next few days, do you?"

"No, why?"

"I'd appreciate it if you could remain available for additional questioning on short notice."

"But of course. I'm happy to help the police in any way I can."

"Would it be a problem for you to call the station once a day and report in?"

Her expression flickered briefly for the first time, but she got it under control again immediately. "No problem."

Nik was relieved that he didn't need to pressure her into it. "Thank you very much. Ms. Ibscher will take you over to have your fingerprints taken now."

Jasmin stood up, and Judith Koch followed her out.

As soon as they closed the door, Nik dialed Sabrina Lampe's number and described Judith Koch to her.

"No," said Sabrina. "That can't possibly be the woman Mrs. Weiss met up with at Pankow Public Park. She sounds like the right age, but from the way Annika Weiss described her, the woman she met in the park looks completely different. Not fat, but not thin either. Slightly overweight, that's how she described her. Brown hair, medium length. More of a tomboy."

No, that couldn't have been Judith Koch, Nik thought. "Unless Mrs. Weiss was lying."

"Can't rule it out. But my gut feeling is that she was telling the truth." Although Sabrina sounded all business, Nik was enjoying listening to her voice. He wanted to talk to her about something besides this case.

"Nik?"

"Yes?"

"Is there anything else?"

Should he ask her out? Was now the right time?

Jasmin returned, carrying a piece of paper.

"No, Sabrina, that's all for now."

"Okay. You've got my number. And this time I'll keep better track of my cell phone."

"Thanks. I'll be in touch."

"Was that Sabrina Lampe?" Jasmin asked.

Why was she grinning at him? "Yeah," he said as he hung up.

"We've got the birthday," she told him, waving the piece of paper she'd brought. It was a copy of a birth certificate notarized by Child Protective Services in the midnineties, during Gerd Lucke's trial. The newborn had been given the name Jennifer Lucke. "But the birthday doesn't match up with any of the women we've been in contact with."

"She'd be around thirty today, too, just like Annika Weiss and Jana Matuschek. Judith Koch, too, come to think of it."

"Yeah, all four of them were born within a period of two and a half years."

"What do you think? How likely is it that the data was changed?

"Usually adopted children just take their new parents' last name, but sometimes they get new first names as well, especially the young ones. Lucke's case was in the papers for weeks. Maybe the adoptive parents were trying to protect the girl by giving her a new first name. I've heard they can theoretically even change someone's birthday if the person is in acute danger," she went on, "although I don't know of any such cases."

"I doubt it applies here. We should find out more about Annika Weiss's, Jana Matuschek's, and Judith Koch's childhoods. Have Thaler and Dombrowski follow up on that."

"I just saw Thaler in the hall. He told me that he talked to Lucke's probation officer."

"And?"

"He said Lucke's behavior has been exemplary."

"That fits with police records. He hasn't been in any trouble since he was last released."

Nik pondered. "What do you think of that Judith Koch?"

His partner summed it up in two words: "Lying snake."

"Too bad her date of birth doesn't match that of Lucke's daughter."

"Their first names both start with *J*, if that means anything. Jennifer and Judith."

"Same with Jana. Probably just a coincidence. Ms. Koch showed us her ID, but I want you to check those details anyway."

"Okay."

"And Florian Lorenz?" Nik asked. "You think he's on the level?"

"Honestly? The guy's too good to be true. Hardworking single parent. Heart of gold."

"Yeah, it's almost hard to believe. People like him only exist in Hallmark movies."

"You watch Hallmark movies?"

"My mother likes to watch them whenever she finds out there's one on. So, is Florian Lorenz for real? Or is there something else to this story with Judith Koch?"

"I have no idea. He seemed genuinely desperate, not like someone who exaggerates. That Koch woman, on the other hand, I wouldn't put anything past her."

"Even murder?"

"Even murder."

"Maybe we should try to lure her out. Confront her with the accusations more aggressively."

"I'd be happy to do that part."

Nik noted to his bemusement that his partner was grinning broadly.

CHAPTER 42

INTERLUDE: *NIGHT TALK,*
101.1 RADIO SPREE ANTENNA

"So, fantastic weather tomorrow. Those of you with the day off, get to the lake. Those of you stuck at the office, stay tuned to 101.1 Radio Spree Antenna. And now it's that time again, just after midnight, and you're listening to *Night Talk* with the She-Wolf."

(Jingle.)

"My name is Franziska Lupa, and I hope you're having a wonderful evening. If not, call me. Hello?"

"Hi."

"Good evening. Who am I speaking to?"

"My name's La—um, Laura."

"Thanks very much for calling, Laura. You sound really young."

"I'm fifteen."

"Okay, Laura. You can call me Franziska, okay?"

"Sure."

"What's on your mind?"

"I listened to *Night Talk* for the first time yesterday. It was about same-sex relationships."

"Are you personally affected by that topic?"

"No, I have a boyfriend."

(Silence.)

"Is this about him?"

"Yeah."

"Is he interested in boys, too?"

"I don't think so."

"But it's about him, you say."

"Yeah."

(Silence.)

"Does he want you to go further than you're ready to?"

"What do you mean, does he want me to go further?"

"Like if he wants to sleep with you and you want to wait. A lot of teenagers have that problem."

"No, we've already slept together. But now he doesn't want to anymore."

"So you want to sleep with him, and he doesn't want to."

"Yeah, exactly."

"And you think maybe he's more into boys?"

"Nah, not that. He's only into me."

"Well, do you know what his problem is?"

"Hair. How fast does it grow back? Is there a way to speed it up?"

"What hair? I'm not sure what you're talking about?"

"The other girls made fun of me when we were showering after gym class. They called it a jungle, said nobody lets theirs grow nowadays. All of them shave down there."

"So then you jumped on the bandwagon?"

"I went out and got disposable razors. I don't get a lot of allowance, and I didn't want to ask my mom about it. Old women don't understand that stuff anyway."

"You didn't hurt yourself, though, did you?"

"No. Everything's fine. But now it itches."

"That's normal when hair grows back. The only way to stop the itching is either to shave regularly or let the hair grow back."

"They said it was more hygienic, too."

"Just the opposite. Your pubic hair provides natural protection against infection. It keeps bacteria from getting into your body. And it keeps the pubic area cool by preventing the skin from rubbing together."

"Yeah, I read all of that on the Internet. But how do I get it to grow back quickly?"

"For your boyfriend?"

"Yeah. He was mad at me for doing it. He said I should have talked to him first. He said it's unnatural and totally unerotic. And . . ."

"Yes?"

"He says it turns him off."

"Oh, dear."

"So? What should I do now?"

"I'm afraid you and your boyfriend are going to have to be patient, Laura."

"Crap."

CHAPTER 43

Researching Judith Koch's childhood brought quick results: she'd grown up with her biological parents, just like Annika Weiss and Jana Matuschek. According to the documentation they found, there was no possibility any of the three women had been adopted as a child.

"Maybe we should do a DNA check just to be a hundred percent sure that none of them are Gerd Lucke's daughter," Jasmin suggested from her seat at the desk across from Nik's.

"I doubt that will tell us anything different, but we should check anyway, yeah."

"I feel like we're still at square one. We still have no idea who this mysterious stranger is."

"Four postcards have gone out so far. Two were followed by murder, one by an attempted murder. How are those three cases connected to Florian Lorenz and Judith Koch?"

There was a knock at the door. "Yeah?" Nik and Jasmin called in unison.

Roland Thaler stuck his head in. "Ms. Koch is here. She's already in the interrogation room."

As Jasmin and Nik entered the room, Judith Koch eyed them suspiciously.

"Why have I been called back in here again?" she asked, crossing her arms. "I told you everything I know." She pressed her lips together.

Nik sat across from her; Jasmin remained standing. "Ms. Koch," she said, "if you like, you're welcome to get an attorney."

"I don't need one."

"In that case, you'll be assigned a public defender. That's normal procedure with murder charges."

Nik hid his surprise. What did Jasmin have up her sleeve?

"Murder?" Judith Koch echoed in disbelief.

"Right. Two counts. We have reason to believe that you, along with another person, planned and carried out two murders. We've just handed the case over to the district attorney. She'll be issuing a warrant for your arrest shortly."

Nik turned to look at his partner. She kept a perfectly straight face. When he turned back to Judith Koch, he saw that her eyelids were twitching. Perhaps she wasn't quite as tough as she acted. "You must be out of your mind," she said, and Nik knew that Jasmin had finally managed to break through Judith's protective shell.

"Two people were brutally murdered. Another person's life was threatened. And you're partially responsible."

"I don't have anything to do with the fact that those pigs got their rightful punishment."

"You can hope for a lighter sentence if you tell us everything you know."

For a moment, Nik thought Judith Koch would finally cave in and tell the truth, but she recovered her composure. "They deserve it. All those rapist pigs ought to be slaughtered."

"Do you mean Mr. Lorenz as well?"

"Please believe me," she said with a lascivious glance up at Niklas. "What?"

"He did it again. He's just like the others."

"Mr. Lorenz raped you again?"

"Yes."

"When?"

"Last night."

"Mr. Lorenz is under police protection. If he'd been anywhere near you, we would know."

At that, her serenity vanished. Beads of sweat formed on her brow. "Am I under arrest now?"

"No."

Without another word, she stood up and left the room.

"Too bad," said Jasmin.

"Yeah, for a while it looked like it might work."

"That woman needs a shrink in the worst way." Jasmin's stomach growled on the way back to their office.

"Want my liverwurst sandwich?" Nik offered. As usual, Elisabeth Steg had packed her son a sandwich and wished him a good day at school. And as usual, Nik handed it off to Jasmin. He hated liverwurst.

CHAPTER 44

Just you wait, Lara.

Sabrina Lampe increased her pace. Yet again, she hadn't found a parking space near her apartment on the west end of Motzstraße. She'd left her car on Viktoria-Luise-Platz and resolved to remember the spot in the morning. Parking was a real headache. Maybe she should look for a spot in an underground garage. That always occurred to her in moments like this. But when she got back home, she would always forget. In any case, her thoughts at the moment were on her daughter.

It was after midnight. Tonight was a school night. Yet Lara had nothing better to do than call some radio host with questions about pubic hair removal!

Sabrina Lampe had no idea why she still listened to that weird Spree Antenna station. It wasn't her type of music. High time she got her CD player repaired. Another resolution that routinely slipped her mind, like finding a parking spot. She'd take care of both tomorrow. Sure she would.

When she reached her apartment building, she looked up. Yep, a light was still on in Lara's window. She was probably watching her hair grow. Or searching for fertilizer online.

At least the ground floor lights were off. And her neighbor, Mrs. Hasselmann, was probably in bed by now, sawing a whole rainforest of logs. At this time of night, she rarely poked her head out the door to call Sabrina's attention to her or Lara's most recent wrongdoings.

Sabrina caught herself tiptoeing up the stairs to make sure they didn't creak, which might call her neighbor to action. No light shone through the keyhole to Lara's room. She must have heard Sabrina opening the apartment door and switched it off. Sabrina walked into her daughter's room and switched on the overhead light.

Lara sat upright and blinked at her mother. "What the—"

"Is this your waking-up act?"

"What do you mean?"

"If I were you, I wouldn't apply to theater school any time soon."

"I was sound asleep!"

"Without turning off your laptop?" The power light was still on.

"So I forgot, so what?"

"And you forgot to turn off the light, too? I saw it from the street just a minute ago."

"Do you work for the NSA now or something? I went to the bathroom. Or is that not allowed anymore?"

Sabrina had read somewhere that the connections in kids' brains rewired themselves during puberty. With Lara she could practically see it happening, live and in real time. And Sabrina prayed that someday soon everything would get plugged back in where it belonged. At least the protests and excuses part of her brain was still firing on all cylinders.

"And you talk in your sleep, too, I suppose?"

"What's that supposed to mean?"

"You called the radio station after midnight. And now all of Berlin knows that you shaved between your legs."

"Whatever. I used a fake name."

"Yeah, *Laura*, very imaginative."

"Why were you even listening to that? Most of the time you've got old-people's music on."

"My CD player is broken." Had she just let herself get provoked into justifying her actions? Her daughter was the one who had explaining to do here. "You know you have a quiz in French tomorrow, right? First period."

"*Mais oui*, madame. So? It's no use anyway."

"Not if you spend your time worrying about shaving your pubic hair."

"Shows what you know."

"Listen, lady, how about you show a little respect. Take a page from Mojito's book."

Had she really just said that? Told her daughter to follow the example of her stick-figure boyfriend who talked about anything and everything? But she couldn't deny that the kid was unfailingly polite and friendly toward her.

"I am. I'm growing it out again."

"You know what? You can style your hair down there however you want. Braid it for all I care. But I don't want you making phone calls after midnight when you have school the next day."

"Okay, fine. Are you going to let me sleep now or what? I have to be rested for French tomorrow."

"Just one other thing," Sabrina said. "Don't you ever call me an old woman again!"

Now she felt better. Much better. She decided she deserved a drink and took a bottle of Bardolino and a glass into the living room. As she sipped her wine, her thoughts drifted back to the *Night Talk* show on Radio Spree Antenna, which she'd been listening to quite a bit lately since her CD player broke.

And then it finally hit her where she'd heard Annika Weiss's voice before, and she understood how it all fit together.

She dialed Niklas Steg's number.

CHAPTER 45

INTERLUDE: *NIGHT TALK,*
101.1 RADIO SPREE ANTENNA

"So the forecast for tomorrow isn't that great. Better take an umbrella. You're listening to 101.1 Radio Spree Antenna. And it's ten past midnight, time for *Night Talk* with the She-Wolf."

(Jingle.)

"My name is Franziska Lupa, and I hope you're having a wonderful evening. If not, call me. Hello?"

(Silence.)

"This is Franziska Lupa, is anyone on the line?"

"Yes."

"Good evening, who's this?"

"You can call me Anna."

"That's not your real name."

"No."

"All right, Anna. Call me Franziska, okay?"

"Okay."

"Wonderful. What's on your mind, Anna?"

"I listen to your show a lot, when I can't sleep. I go into the kitchen and turn the radio on. Low volume, so it doesn't wake my husband."

"Are you calling because of something to do with your husband?"

(Silence.)

"Yeah."

"If he woke up and found you in the kitchen, would there be a problem?"

"Depends."

"On what?"

"On what kind of mood he was in."

"Does he drink?"

"No."

"But he's unpredictable?"

"Yeah."

"Before we continue, is he asleep in the other room right now?"

"No, he's gone out. If he comes back, I'll hang up immediately."

"Does he leave in the middle of the night a lot?"

"From time to time."

"And you don't know where he goes? Is that the problem?"

"No, I know where he is. He takes his things with him."

"What things?"

"Leather things."

"Leather things?"

"You know, masks and collars and whips and stuff."

"You two are active in the S and M scene?"

"No, well, yeah."

"What do you mean?"

"I don't go with him."

"I hear a shudder in your voice."

"It's just not normal, is it?"

"If both partners are okay with it, there's nothing wrong with it."

(Silence.)

"But you're not okay with it, am I right?"

"I think it's perverse."

"So he goes out by himself regularly, yeah? To clubs? To a dominatrix?"

(Caller laughs.)

"A dominatrix? No, he's the one who needs to be able to beat someone up. Otherwise, he can't get it up anymore."

"And he's—excuse the pun—hitting other locations for what he's not getting at home?"

"Not just that."

"What else?"

(Silence.)

"He whips me."

(Silence.)

"He's put brackets into the wall in our bedroom so he can tie my arms up. And then he starts hitting me. If I scream, he puts a gag in my mouth."

(Silence.)

"I can't take it anymore. Last time I couldn't lie on my back for a week afterward. And . . ."

"What else?"

"He uses me."

"Can you be more specific?"

"He penetrates me from behind while I'm tied up and bleeding."

"How long has this been going on?"

"Two and a half years."

"Anna, you need to seek help immediately. I don't think I'm the right person to talk to about this."

(Caller begins to cry.)

"Anna, you have to end this relationship. By whatever means possible."

"I know."

CHAPTER 46

The woman checked one more time that the Makarov was loaded before putting it into her purse, along with her cell phone. No doubt about it, Dominik Weiss got what he deserved. Moritz Schütte, too. Such a tragedy, though, that Jana Matuschek took her own life. Such a pretty young woman. Why couldn't she have just waited?

Did she not make it clear enough that Schütte would get his rightful punishment? That the public would see that Jana Matuschek was innocent and Schütte a monster who deserved to die?

The woman didn't trust men in general anyway.

She'd tried getting involved with one as a teenager. And in her early twenties, she tried a second time. But both times she'd made a hasty retreat. The sight of a naked man had been too much for her. It immediately conjured up images of her father, nude, touching himself and staring at her shamelessly.

But that had been a long time ago, in a former life, when her last name had still been Lucke. She'd blocked the name from her mind for many years. Until this spring, when she'd actually crossed paths with her father. Unlike his surname, she'd never been able to forget his face.

How could she, when she saw it in the face of every man who tried to come near her or flirt with her?

She'd followed her father to his residence that day he happened to walk past her on Kurfürstendamm. Saw the name Lucke next to one of the doorbells.

And Jennifer Lucke was the name on the documents the government office had sent her later on. A name that held no meaning for her anymore. And yet it had once been hers. If only her mother hadn't . . . She pushed away the image of the woman hanging from the ceiling, the memory of herself as a little girl, looking up at her in fear.

Frustrating that things hadn't gone according to plan. Extremely frustrating. She'd thought Annika Weiss would be capable of it. After that, the woman had resolved to take care of things herself.

The way she had with Moritz Schütte. Should she have let Jana Matuschek know in advance? Perhaps then she'd still be alive. But it wasn't her fault, no, certainly not. It was Schütte's fault. And the fault of the justice system that failed to deliver justice to these rapist pigs. Including this Florian Lorenz that Judith Koch had told her about. He'd raped her repeatedly. Judith Koch had cried when she told her about it. She'd gone to the police, too.

And the police? They believed a rapist. Again. Lorenz had even had the nerve to press charges himself. Stalking, he said. But Judith Koch had only wanted to talk to him, to clear things up. She'd even been willing to forgive him and give him another chance. Which the woman could not fathom for a moment. Once a rapist, always a rapist. There was only one solution: render them harmless.

The pistol in the woman's purse was loaded, and Florian Lorenz was going to get what he deserved. Today.

CHAPTER 47

Nik and Jasmin arrived at the Radio Spree Antenna building just before eight in the morning. A station employee let them in after they showed him their badges. He led them into a conference room and said he'd have coffee sent in. And he referred them to the press speaker, who fortunately arrived only a few minutes later.

The woman welcomed the detectives warmly and introduced herself as Uta Trommele. "Ms. Ibscher, Mr. Steg," she said with a friendly smile. "What can I do for you?" Like every press speaker Nik had ever met, Ms. Trommele clearly made a point of putting on a happy face.

"Are you aware of the series of murders the police are investigating at the moment?"

"Reap the storm?"

Nik nodded.

"Awful, just awful." Her expression grew solemn for a moment as she feigned compassion, but then she went right back to smiling ingratiatingly at the two detectives. "We here at Spree Antenna have been covering the story extensively as well. Any news?"

"Possibly. That's why we're here."

"What do you mean?"

"We have reason to believe that one or more suspicious persons called into one of your shows. To *Night Talk*, specifically."

"They called Ms. Lupa?"

"Right. We presume that you have recordings of those programs, and we'd like to give them a listen."

"Do you have a search warrant?" Her facial expression didn't change—she clearly had years of practice.

"No, we just got the information last night." Nik thought back to Sabrina Lampe's phone call, to the agitated, tense sound of her normally cheerful voice. "We've contacted the judge and expect to hear back any minute now."

"Without an official search warrant, I really can't just hand you the Spree Antenna program recordings." Uta Trommele was still smiling; her tone was as cheerfully bland as if she'd just told them she'd had granola for breakfast. Nik thought he heard a trace of a Bavarian accent in her vowels.

"Let me clarify," Jasmin spoke up. "You can either let us listen to the recordings here at the station—we won't take anything with us—and if nothing comes of our suspicions, nobody will know we were here. If they're confirmed, then we'll make sure to commend your cooperation publicly." Then Jasmin's expression went from friendly to threatening. "Or we could let the press know that our investigations led us to Radio Spree Antenna and they refused to assist us."

The press secretary's face didn't change.

"This is about murder," Nik added. "And every second counts. If we had time to wait for the official paperwork to go through, we would."

"Do you want to end up sharing the blame?" Jasmin asked, appealing to her sense of moral responsibility.

Although her demeanor remained cheerfully bland, Nik sensed that Ms. Trommele was carefully weighing the alternatives. She decided the potential damage to the station's reputation was not worth the risk. "All right then," she said, still smiling. "I'll take you into the recording studio and ask one of our engineers to give you the tapes you're looking for."

"Thank you very much," Nik said, and not ten minutes later, he and Jasmin were adjusting their headphones as a sound engineer queued up the first recording. They spent the morning listening to sleepless callers' problems and Franziska Lupa's thoughtful replies. Wives with cheating husbands, lovers with erectile dysfunction, pubescent youths, people frustrated in one way or another with their lives. Jasmin's face repeatedly registered disapproval bordering on disgust.

When they heard Sabrina's daughter's call, Nik had to grin. Maybe he'd meet Lara someday—if he ever managed to talk to Sabrina on the phone for reasons other than police business.

He saw Jasmin flinch when a caller on the next tape—recorded earlier, Nik noted, so the engineer must have got the sequence mixed up—introduced herself. She called herself Anna, and then Nik recognized the voice as well: it was Annika Weiss, no doubt about it. And the masks, whips, and gags this Anna was describing fit exactly with what they'd seen at the crime scene. Sabrina had been right.

The missing link connecting the murders was right here at Radio Spree Antenna. Minutes later they heard Judith Koch call in with her own contrived tale of woe. Nik and Jasmin were confident they'd find a connection to Jana Matuschek, too. But a call from Roland Thaler kept them from continuing their search.

"You requested a search warrant for Radio Spree Antenna? It just got approved."

"Don't need it anymore," Nik said. "They let us in voluntarily."

"And we just got the results back on our search for Jennifer Lucke's adoptive parents."

"Yeah?"

"She was adopted by a couple whose last name was Lupa. We don't know yet if the Lupas changed Jennifer's first name as well."

"Franziska."

"Excuse me?"

"We just came across her name ourselves. She's the reason we're here at the station."

After that, things started happening very quickly. Upon learning that the court had authorized the search warrant, the press secretary decided to cooperate fully with the police and provided Franziska Lupa's home address.

Nik and Jasmin got to her place at the same time as the unit Nik had sent there. No one answered the door when they pounded on it. Nik had the two officers break it open.

The radio host was nowhere to be found, but if they'd needed any further proof that they were on the right track, they had it now, in the form of a portrait photo of Franziska Lupa in the living room. Nik and Jasmin both recognized her as a spectator who'd been present at Moritz Schütte's trial.

Realizing that Florian Lorenz was in immediate danger, he called Emma Dombrowski, who had been sent to his apartment to protect him.

Officer Dombrowski didn't respond.

CHAPTER 48

Franziska Lupa dialed Florian Lorenz's number. He answered the phone, and she hung up right away.

Yes, he was at home.

Foremost in Franziska's mind was stopping the man from doing to his two daughters what her father, Gerd Lucke, had done to her. But it was equally important to her that the girls not witness the violence. Judith Koch had assured her that Lorenz's mother had picked the girls up that morning.

And if Judith Koch had any sense, she was no longer in the vicinity. Franziska had instructed her to create an airtight alibi. If the woman had followed her advice, she was currently surrounded by as many people as possible, people who could later confirm she'd been nowhere near the scene of the crime.

The door to Lorenz's apartment building was propped open. Franziska Lupa stepped inside and took the stairs to the fourth floor. After a couple of deep breaths, she took the gun from her purse and rang the doorbell.

To her surprise, a woman answered the door.

Absolutely unbelievable. He'd already started luring in his next victim!

The woman in the doorway stared at her in confusion; presumably she had a similar look on her own face.

The other woman was the first to regain her composure. "Drop your weapon!" she ordered.

The self-anointed angel of vengeance wasn't about to do that. Her thoughts raced as she considered the best course of action under the unexpected circumstances. Florian Lorenz appearing in the background distracted her, making it more difficult to think clearly about the situation. She'd resolved to kill him, and she intended to do so. He deserved it.

The image of her father, staring at her lustfully, with her mother hanging from the ceiling, pushed its way to the forefront of her consciousness. She'd seen that same look on Dominik Weiss's face before he realized it wasn't his wife in front of him wearing the mask. Moritz Schütte's sick lust hadn't had time to surface before she shot him.

Her father, Gerd Lucke, the man responsible for it all, would soon draw his last breath as well—of this she was certain. She didn't care what happened to her. Just as long as all the other women out there learned it was not only appropriate but essential for them to take matters into their own hands. Lupa hoped to serve as a shining example for all sexually abused women.

The woman blocking her way took advantage of Lupa's brief moment of distraction by lunging forward in an attempt to knock the assailant's weapon aside.

Detective Dombrowski's attempt was only partly successful. Instinctively, Lupa pulled the trigger. Nothing was going to stop her from getting her revenge.

Dombrowski screamed; her blouse turned red. She struggled to keep her balance. Hurriedly, Lupa shoved the woman to the ground and stepped around her. She aimed the gun at Florian Lorenz.

Should she just shoot him right now? No. He needed to know why he was about to die. And he needed to die slowly, in excruciating pain, the way he deserved.

Sometimes it's important to do things that have to be done.

She heard a vibrating noise. It was coming from the other woman. Probably her cell phone. Lupa ignored it along with the woman's injury. Couldn't be all that bad, she hoped. At any rate, the woman no longer seemed to pose a danger. Apart from the fact that she'd seen Franziska's face. But so what if she had? She planned to go directly to her father's place just as soon as this man was brought to justice.

She directed Florian Lorenz into the bedroom.

CHAPTER 49

When he saw Officer Dombrowski hit the floor, Florian Lorenz knew he was alone with the crazed-looking assailant. Dombrowski stared up at him in disbelief for a moment before closing her eyes. The other woman strode toward him, pushing the door closed behind her while keeping her gun aimed straight at his heart. He shrank back against the frame of the bedroom door. The woman waved her weapon to indicate that he should go inside.

"We need to call an ambulance."

"That won't do you any good."

"She needs medical attention."

"I'll take care of her when I'm done with you." She swept her gaze around the room. "So this is where it happened."

"Where what happened?"

"This is where you raped the women."

"What? What women?"

"I know everything. The woman that was shot will be thankful that I stopped you in time."

"What are you talking about?"

The expression in her eyes seemed familiar to him.

"About justice. And about making sure a jury won't end up acquitting you."

Florian was stupefied. He didn't have a clue what she was talking about.

"Judith Koch told me everything."

"Judith! I should have realized."

"Too late for that, scumbag."

"Listen, I don't know who you are or how you know Judith, but believe me, she's lying. She lies every time she opens her mouth."

"Yeah, right. Rape victims always lie. You've gotten a lot of mileage in court using that defense. But all that's going to change. Soon none of you will get away with it any longer. We are many, and we stick together."

Suddenly it came to him whose eyes hers reminded him of.

"Clothes off," she ordered.

His aunt Elvira's eyes. She'd suffered from a persecution complex, thought she was surrounded by members of some ominous "ring." The customer behind her in line at the bank, the couple who walked past her in the park, the man who came to her apartment to read the gas meter, they were all part of the "ring." No therapy or medication had helped. She'd spent the last years of her life in the psychiatric ward at Charité hospital.

"Don't make me repeat myself. Clothes off!"

If this madwoman was anything like his aunt Elvira, he knew it was futile to reason with her or appeal to her common sense. He pulled off his T-shirt.

The pistol with its long silencer was pointed at his bare chest. "Lose the pants."

Whether she was crazy or not, his only hope was to attempt to reason with her.

"Listen to me! It's not too late. We can still call an ambulance. If that police officer bleeds to death, you'll be charged with murder."

"Police officer? That's a good one."

"She was posted here for my protection."

The woman laughed. "For your protection? What kind of world is this, where rapists get protection?"

"Please, you have to believe me. I didn't rape Judith. I didn't rape anyone. She's making all of this up."

"Oh, yeah? And none of the other pigs raped anyone, either, I suppose? All the other women were making it up, too?"

And all at once, Florian knew beyond doubt that this was the woman the police were searching for. The same woman who'd sent the postcard.

"Sow the wind . . . ," he whispered.

"Lose the pants, I said."

Time. He needed time. He needed to make her believe him, even though he remembered how futile communication with his aunt had been.

Slowly he began unzipping his pants. His hands were shaking of their own volition, and he feigned that his zipper was stuck.

"I could just shoot you right now."

Despite his fear, he forced himself to pull the zipper down as slowly as possible. Maybe one of the neighbors had heard something. Should he call for help? No, the woman would pull the trigger immediately.

"Hurry up! Now the belt."

There was no need for pretense now. His fingers were trembling so badly that he had genuine difficulty unbuckling his belt.

"I told you to hurry up!"

His pants dropped to his ankles. The woman's expression told him she was taking immense satisfaction in his terror.

"Shoes off, then pants."

He kicked off his slippers and removed his pants. He was down to his socks and underwear.

She lowered her weapon, aiming at his genitals.

"I want to see it in front of me."

"What?"

"I want to see it when I deactivate it."

"Please believe me. I didn't do anything. Judith is lying. You have to believe me."

"Underwear off. Socks, too."

Florian thought he saw her twitch impatiently, ready to pull the trigger.

He needed to buy more time. He did as she ordered but drew it out, praying not to appear obvious.

"You're all animals. Switch your brains off. Let your instincts take over."

Now he was standing naked before her.

"Do you admit to having raped women?"

He was silent.

"Do you agree that you deserve appropriate punishment?"

He resigned himself to his fate. Nothing could dissuade her.

Suddenly he heard a crash.

Not the dreaded gunshot. The noise had come from out in the hall.

The expression on the woman's face changed to alarm.

Maybe now he . . . ? A chance . . . ?

Her rapid blinking revealed her mounting agitation.

If he was going to make a move, it had to be now.

He took a step toward her, reaching for her gun hand.

Her finger twitched, her hand made an uncontrolled movement, and the pain hit him instantly. He looked down at himself in disbelief and saw blood spurting out from his body.

Then everything went black.

CHAPTER 50

"Dombrowski isn't answering," Nik said. Jasmin's expression told him warning sirens were going off in her head, too. Without another word, they hurried out of Franziska Lupa's apartment, mounted the flashing light on their car, and sped toward Florian Lorenz's address. Nik called the station and requested urgent backup and an ambulance, sirens off in the hope the suspect wouldn't panic. Jasmin hit the gas. "We'll be there in ten minutes," she said, and drove hell-bent for leather.

They screeched to a stop in front of Florian Lorenz's building. A man was standing there with his wirehaired dachshund beside him on a leash. Both man and dachshund stared in bewilderment as Nik and Jasmin scrambled out of the car and ran into the building. Jasmin beat him to the fourth-floor apartment and was kicking in the door when Nik caught up to her. Nik drew his gun.

Dombrowski was lying in still-fresh blood on the floor in front of them. The shooter, they deduced, might still be nearby. Their first priority had to be the shooter.

Nik positioned himself just outside an open door to another room. Jasmin covered him as he threw himself against the doorframe and aimed his gun into the room.

And there she was, the woman in the photo, the woman who counseled desperate souls on the radio: Franziska Lupa. She was holding a gun as well, and her expression was one of utter determination. Her gun was pointed at Florian Lorenz, who was just taking a step in her direction.

Without hesitating, Nik fired. The bullet hit the back of the woman's hand, sending her pistol flying against a wall.

That Lupa had shot Florian Lorenz was evident from the blood spurting from a wound in his pelvic area. The man collapsed in a heap. Jasmin immediately forced Lupa's arms behind her back and handcuffed her.

Nik hurried to the injured man. He had to stop the bleeding. There was no time to lose.

"I'll take care of Dombrowski," Jasmin said.

Nik ripped off a section of his shirt and pressed it tightly against Lorenz's wound. Should he roll the man into a stable position on his side? Or would that do more harm than good? Before Nik could decide, several paramedics hurried into the room and took over.

Only now did Nik turn his attention back to Franziska Lupa. She had made no attempt to flee, just stood there looking on.

"The bullet only grazed the inside of his thigh," said one of the paramedics. "Looks worse than it is." The paramedic tending to Emma Dombrowski gave an all-clear signal as well: no life-threatening injuries. Nik realized they had arrived just in time.

Franziska Lupa's expression was one of disappointment. It remained that way as Jasmin read her her rights and led her out.

CHAPTER 51

Why, of all places, Nik asked himself, had he chosen the beer garden on Lake Wannsee as the location for their get-together?

Sabrina still refused to call it a date, the way her daughter, Lara, did. She and Mojito had discussed it in Sabrina's presence, and Lara had emphasized the word *date* with a grin at her mother. No one, thankfully, brought up the topic of shaved genitalia. How ironic, thought Sabrina, that Lara's call to *Night Talk* had jogged Sabrina's memory about where she'd heard Annika Weiss's voice. Otherwise, Florian Lorenz would probably be dead. Nik thought so, too. He was sitting across from Sabrina and had just finished summarizing the events of the past few days from a police standpoint.

They'd ordered coffee and sat facing beautiful Lake Wannsee. The sun was high in the cloudless sky, shimmering on the surface of the water. Several sailboats were out, and off in the distance, they could see a passenger steamship heading toward Potsdam.

The embarrassing incident that had befallen her cell phone a few weeks before had happened on that steamship, or one like it. She wasn't sure she wanted to tell Nik about it.

"If you hadn't tipped us off about *Night Talk*," Nik was saying, "things would have turned out much worse. We're really in your debt, Sabrina."

She enjoyed his distinctive bass voice. Hearing him call her by her first name in such a romantic setting secretly thrilled her.

"I only wish we could have prevented Jana Matuschek's suicide," Nik said.

"Poor Ms. Matuschek," Sabrina agreed. "You know, if something like that happened to me, or if someone did that to my daughter . . ." She paused and reflected a moment before continuing. "I can't say that I wouldn't go after the guy myself. Even if it meant going to jail."

She expected Nik to contradict her. To say you couldn't take the law into your own hands, you have to trust the police and the justice system. But Nik just listened.

"And then to be humiliated in court, the way you described. When I think about guys like Moritz Schütte getting away with rape, being free to roam the streets again—in a certain sense, I can understand where Franziska Lupa was coming from."

"Well, her crimes can be explained, but that doesn't mean they can be excused. We can't tolerate vigilantism. She killed two people in horrible ways."

"With Florian Lorenz, she risked putting his daughters through similar trauma to what she experienced as a child," Sabrina added thoughtfully.

"I'm not sure she was aware of that," Nik said. "And even if she was, her insanity trumped everything else. Judging by the initial conversations we've had with her, she has an extremely obsessive personality with no tolerance for counterarguments. Ms. Lupa didn't just believe she was in the right. She called it her 'sacred duty.' No question, she would have kept on killing, probably with fewer inhibitions each time."

"Is she competent to stand trial?"

"I have my doubts there. Right now she's being held at a psychiatric hospital. It will all be decided later."

"There's one thing I still have a hard time believing."

"What's that?"

"Gerd Lucke. Shouldn't he have been able to recognize his daughter?"

"Yeah. He's since admitted that he knew who his stalker was. His plan was to get you to find out her address for him. Then he was going to solve the problem his way, whatever that would have been."

"What an awful man," Sabrina said. She looked into Nik's eyes and thought just the opposite about him. He smiled at her, and she felt her knees go weak.

"Do you know why I never answered your texts?"

"No, but I have to admit that I was quite disappointed by it."

She turned away, went back to watching the sunlight glittering on the gentle waves of Lake Wannsee. "This woman had hired me to shadow her husband. I'd tailed him out here, to Wannsee station. Then he boarded one of the tour boats, and I followed him. It was a day like today—hot, sunny, lots of people out and about. And I caught him in the act, kissing his girlfriend. I pulled my phone out of my pocket and leaned out over the railing a little so that I could get them both in the picture." She'd never told anyone this story before; it was just too embarrassing. "A little boy bumped into me."

"And?"

She pointed out into the distance. "It's out there now, that phone. At the bottom of the lake. Along with all the contact information I'd saved on it."

She could never let Mojito find out about that. He'd just lecture her about polluting the environment.

She'd actually expected Nik to laugh at her, but he only grinned. "You could have reached me at the station."

Sabrina was elated that he didn't sound reproachful. "Yeah, I wanted to."

"But?"

"I hadn't gathered up the courage yet." She sipped her coffee.

"One more reason why it was useful that I brought you on board for the Annika Weiss case."

She didn't even try to hold back the smile that lit up her face.

He smiled broadly in return. "What do you think, Sabrina? Will we have to wait until the next case to see each other again, or can we manage it sooner?"

"Sooner, Nik, I'm sure."

For Sabrina Lampe, it was a truly wonderful, sunny day at the lake.

And now she was certain that it was only going to get better.

ABOUT THE AUTHOR

Photo © 2014 Daniela Mair

Siegfried Langer was born in Memmingen, Germany. He spent eighteen years in Berlin before returning to his hometown in 2014. His first novel, *Alles bleibt anders* (*Everything Stays Different*), was nominated for the Kurd Laßwitz and Deutscher Phantastik Prizes. His thrillers include *Vater, Mutter, Tod* (*Father, Mother, Death*), *Sterbenswort* (*Dead Silence*), and *Leide!* (*Suffer!*). *Reap the Storm* is his English debut.

ABOUT THE TRANSLATOR

Photo © 2012 Melissa Steckbauer

Jaime McGill was born in Omaha, Nebraska, and has been living and freelancing in Berlin, Germany, since 2005. Language, music, and travel are her three great passions, so she is happiest when translating novels while on the road with one of her bands. Previous literary projects include works by van Deus (*Operation Solstice Ten*, *The Steps of Evil*, and *The Ampullae of Lorenzini*), Katrin Bongard's *Loving*, and Miranda J. Fox's *Next Stop: Love*.